THE CHRONICLES OF PIRAH

Book II: To the Halls of the Old Gods and the Great Houses of Men

EARL FAIRFEILD

The Chronicles of Pirah

Book II: To the Halls of the Old Gods and the Great Houses of Men

© 2021 Earl Fairfeild

All rights reserved. No part of this publication may be reproduced, distributed, or transmitted in any form or by any means, including photocopying, recording, or other electronic or mechanical methods, without the prior written permission of the publisher, except in the case brief quotations embodied in critical reviews and other noncommercial uses permitted by copyright law.

ISBN:
Paperback   978-1-63945-293-4
E-book   978-1-63945-294-1

The views expressed in this book are solely those of the author and do not necessarily reflect the views of the publisher, and the publisher hereby disclaims any responsibility for them.

Writers' Branding
1800-608-6550
www.writersbranding.com
orders@writersbranding.com

CONTENTS

CHAPTER 1:
Hymmnaught Has Fallen 1

CHAPTER 2
Zu: Villain, Vile, Victor..13

CHAPTER 3:
Pirah 27

CHAPTER 4:
Alitius 39

CHAPTER 5
The Oath of Feckulis, the Mikro Vadakos, Pirah Means to Strike 49

CHAPTER 6
The Gods..59

CHAPTER 7
Ogres, Celoth, Vessiel's Wrath..75

CHAPTER 8
Feckulis No More 85

CHAPTER 9
The Great Houses of Men..93

CHAPTER 10
A Reckoning, a God Crushed, an Unholy Alliance...............109

CHAPTER 11
Student, Disciple, Lord...121

CHAPTER I

Hymmnaught Has Fallen

Hymmnaught lay semiconscious in his chambers, several attendants standing about, awaiting commands from the higher-ranking Ogres that stood beside him. Grievous were his wounds as they had taken their toll on the King of Growgothal, who fought off the enemy that sought to destroy his city. All were dour and of foul mood, for they could not do any more than watch as their King struggled with his last breaths. The physicians of Growgothal did not have the skills of most other realms, for Ogres will endure their pain while healing with strong drink and even stronger will. There would be no healing for Hymmnaught.

The remaining higher members of Hymmnaught's council stood in powerless disbelief that their King had fallen, for in the hearts and minds of all who dwelled in Growgothal, there was no one mightier than he. No one in the room felt this more than one who sat beside him, holding his rough and bloodied hand, staring into his eyes, and fighting back tears the Ogress Vessiel, Queen of Growgothal, mate to Hymmnaught, and mother of his twenty-four children. The great King of Growgothal fought hard and fiercely in the battle for his city and kingdom, and loe, did he slay many of the Celoth that were thought to claim the life of the King of Ogres in face-to-face combat, but this was not to be, for all that came within his mighty reach fell like wheat before the scythe. Loud and terrifying was his roar, and strong were his soldiers in their rally for the King they served, but to no avail, for the numbers they fought seem to grow and grow without end. The Borians came down from their high formations and lay into the Ogre ranks with Dragon's Fire depleting the forces that protected the Ogre realm. Though the air did reek of burned flesh and the sounds clanging weapons and shouts of the brutes mingled with the snarls of Ogres, the battle surely seemed to be going the way of the enemy. The city was now burning in some places, for the ballistas and trebuchet had been destroyed. A mass of Celoth did charge the now wide-open gates, only to meet the citizenry of the Capital of Growgothal all armed with axes and clubs, seething with rage and lust for battle for Ogres, be they warrior or commoner, are not a timid breed.

When it would seem that it would take but one great charge and the Celoth would overwhelm the Ogres, there was a mighty roar from the skies that could be heard for miles about. *"Argain!"* was the war cry of the Dragon realm, of which Serous Drakkus was King; they came from above as the forces he dispatched had arrived and wasted no time joining the battle. The massive Dragons of Argain dashed into the formations of the Borian host, engaging Dragon to Dragon with claw and fang, for Dragon's Fire had little effect on any actual Dragon save scorching and irritation but perhaps rending the rider in this case to ashes. The battle in the air brought roars of gratitude from the Ogres, now not having to dodge the strafing runs of the Borians. The Celoth, on the other hand, had to resort to tactics of their own to avoid being incinerated. The battle had begun to turn, but was it too late for the capitol? The Argain Dragons divided into two groups one to attack the Borian host and the other to attack the Celoth hoard below. The Ogres, still fighting among the Brutes, were too busy being involved with their favorite distraction life-and-death fighting to observe the welcomed arrival of allies from the sky; however, the commanders of the now present Ogre contingent having finally arrived from parts all over Growgothal did and ordered that the horns be blown in signal of retreat and regroup.

As savage and enraged as the Ogres were, they did obey the commands and formed into arched shield walls, all the while fighting blow for blow with an equally determined adversary. The Celoth, trying ever harder, remain mingled with the Ogres so as to keep the Argain from incinerating them before they could make their escape, for the object was not to win and conquer… but to engage in and create mayhem and destruction and slay all those dear to the enemies of their God King. With that sole idea in mind, the Celoth commander gave orders for the forces not engaged in fighting to muster in positions ready for portal and to signal the Borian riders to disengage and make their egress.

With this accomplished with banner and horns, the Celoth still fighting knew at once that they would be made sacrifice to allow for the escape of their comrades. A lone lieutenant among the Celoth looked back at his commander, who met his gaze and gave a simple nod. The junior officer raised his sword over his head in salute and roared his last command.

"Death is ours. Make them pay for it!" The Celoth still fighting formed a sickle before the Ogres, jabbing and slashing with all they had as the reserves formed and began entering the newly created portals made large enough to send them charging twenty abreast. The Ogres became even more determined to crush the enemy and deny those trying to escape entrance to the portals, for they had not received their vengeance—not yet at least. For it was only but a moment when the Argain dove down upon them in rows of four, smashing the formations of the Celoth with tail and claw separating the two hoards and then a second wave with full bellows exhaling the horrifying Dragon's fire into enemies, incinerating all that were left that did not enter the portals. Little that there was, once again the enemy had the day, for the damage that was done reached deeply into the capital of Growgothal and far greater than they had suffered.

Closer to the capital gate that was now destroyed stood Hymmnaught, clutching the butt end of his great ax with both hands, the head pushed to the ground as he steadied himself. A terrifying scowl was across the face of the King of Growgothal, for his kingdom had been attacked, and the preparations they had made barely stood against the enemy, and he felt rage in his heart. Alas, his rage was not merely for the battle, but what he knew was the fate he had been dealt on this day. Many piercings from arrows did he receive, and so did they protrude from his chest and back, and though they took their toll, they were nothing as to the

Dragon lance that had passed through him at the waist. He did not even feel the weapon made to fell a Dragon in flight; so great was his lust for battle, his Ogre's rage. Yet the damage had been done. The lance still embedded in the King of Ogres was his undoing; he knew that he was finished, and there would be no vengeance for Hymmnaught.

Not by the hand of the King of Ogres at least, for one must not forget that there were many scores of Ogres left in the Kingdom of Growgothal, and Ogres as one should know, were not a timid breed.

And so did Hymmnaught lie in his bed, not fully conscious for he had lost a great amount of blood, yet he clutched his ax as if to take it with him when he would transcend to the next world. Such were the beliefs of the Ogres, as was for many of the life-forms of the Mystic realm, for there may be many battles to fight on the other side, where the Greater Powers dwelled. It was believed that if anyone entering the other side not properly armed will be tossed into the great void without name or claim, to land in some place, left to his or her own devices. Hymmnaught would not disappoint the Greater Powers if that were the case.

Vessiel looked up to one of the ranking generals and spoke. "Xacton, what of the physicians we did request? Are those from Avalon to portal or fly at their best?"

General Xacton replied with a tinge of frustration. "Me thinks that flight be the only choice, for the spell that was cast is strong indeed. As you know, we lack the magic that we need." The despair in the room grew as the breathing of Hymmnaught became weaker and weaker. General Xacton gave orders to find the Ogre Mystic once again for him try to break the spell that prevented any allies from portal traveling to the capitol.

The aide at his side relayed the orders to the royal guards just outside the King's quarters, and all made haste to do their general's biding. The guards did not have far to look for the Mystic, for he was hard at work just outside the main gates, conjuring and using great gestures to rebuild the gates that had been destroyed. He was called Bosurous, he that had learned the Mystic arts from Pirah and those that Pirah had taught before him in the days of the first age on Earth Mother. Though Bosurous indeed was skilled, alas, he did not possess the ability to heal his King or fend off great armies with such magic as the Old One or Serous Drakkus, for he above all was an Ogre with an Ogre's patience, or lack thereof. His ability to restore objects to their former state was, however, excellent. As he was working on restoring the gates, a royal guard approached and spoke in the Ogre tongue. "Lord Mystic, General Xacton bids you pull a spell from your arse and crush that which keeps any from making portal to the capitol." Said the Captain of the Royal Guards.

He replied, "I would have much better luck pulling such a spell from the arse of the Lord

General, for all the good it will do. The spell that blocks one and all was placed by a very powerful Mystic, one with power greater than my own. We will need the power of the Avalon or even Pirah himself. The Argain have dispatched a platoon of their swiftest to bring back those physicians our King so desperately needs. We can only wait, Captain."

At that moment, there was a great rumbling sound that seemed to build momentum and then stop. The Ogres all looked about as they pulled their weapons, all but Bosurous, who knew what magic was happening. He looked about, trying to find a sign the source of where it could be manifesting, but to no avail. With a deafening *crack* and a brief flash of light, there was a massive distortion in the air not but a hundred feet from where the Ogres stood by the gate, as though something were trying to get through an invisible wall, smashing into it with immense power. "Stay your weapons!" bellowed Bosurous, for only a friend could be trying to smash through the spell a very powerful friend.

With yet another deafening *crack!*, the distortion became much more apparent and visible to the Ogres, that now watched with anticipation to see what would come through this forced portal. The city dwellers and warriors that were working about the walls stopped what they were doing, having been roused by the sound of impact. Once again, the powerful noise struck the now visible impact point with such force, the fabric of the Mystic realm at that place shattered and sent shards of plasma and other destroyed fragments of elements that had the misfortune of being present during the onslaught, the great force throwing the Ogres back several feet, knocking them to the ground.

As the debris settled, there was the sound of thundering hoofs and the shouts of what sounded like men and women. Bosurous stumbled while rising from the ground; he cleared the dust from his eyes and looked about to see that he and the king's guard were surrounded by several hundred Centaurs, the commander of which cantered up to Bosurous, removed his helmet, and spoke. "I am Corian, Captain of this host. I bring physicians and medicine for the King of Ogres. We must go to him at once. Make haste, *damn you!*"

The Ogres all at once jumped in the direction of the main gates that had not been fully reconstructed. Bosurous made a wide gesture, and the gates were brushed aside. The Centaurs galloped behind them and thus were slowed by their two-legged allies. The Ogre captain halted and spoke to Corian. "Follow the road for it will lead. We cannot match a Centaur's speed. There is no time for us to waste. Go now, Captain! Indeed, *make haste*!"

The Centaurs, as one, charged down the road that led to Hymmnaught's palace the, sound of their hoofs echoing throughout the city. The dwellers of the city were jumping aside as Corian called out, "Make way for the sake Hymmnaught!"

The host of the Centaurs approached the palace of the King and took position as the first ten continued to Hymmnaught's chamber. The Centauresses and Centaurs that made up the group of physicians rushed through the halls that lead to Hymmnaught along with the Royal Guards. As they approached the entrance to the royal chamber, the mood was somber. Indeed, Corian entered first to see that the King of Ogres was about to draw his last breath. The Centaur captain motioned for the physicians to set forth and revive him, but it was for naught. The King, so mighty in his days, gasped a deep and long inhalation, his eyes opening wide and looking squarely into the face Vessiel, his beloved wife and Queen.

He whispered to her in the tongue of Ogres as she bent over him and looked back at her dying husband and King, her eyes filling with tears. he simply nodded and placed her forehead on his in Ogre fashion. He then slumped back in his bed, his last breath leaving his body, his ax still clutched in both hands. Hymmnaught, King of Growgothal, did transcend to the next realm. The Ogres in the chamber bowed their heads, as did the Centaurs, but only for a moment. As one, the Ogres drew their weapons and raised both arms above their heads, looking to the sky beyond the ceiling, and let out an ear-piercing roar that became a howl that lasted for an extended moment, a warning to the next realm that an Ogre King had come.

The room then emptied, all but Vessiel, who lingered for some time after her beloved Hymmnaught passed, staring at his now lifeless form. She wiped the tears from her face and took a deep breath, then stood. She took one last longing look at the great beast that had won her heart and became her mate for life by Ogre tradition of combat, forsaking all other females just for her, rising to the throne of Growgothal, and loving her in Ogre fashion as well as their twenty-four offspring.

She stepped from the chamber and was met by stewards that would carry his body to the cleansing mausoleum, where it would be washed and prepared for the great funeral pyre that would be placed upon higher ground than the rest, for he was King. Vessiel looked to the Centaur Captain and spoke in the common tongue. "I am grateful you did break the spell that blocked the way to us, but tell how come you, friends of hoof and hair that burst the fabric of the Mystic fare?"

Corian placed his hand to his breastplate and bowed his head slightly to the Queen of Ogres. He looked with dismay as the attendants carried the body of Hymmnaught past. He then looked to Vessiel and spoke. "Upon arriving at sacred Avalon, my commander bid me to gather troops and physicians to go to Growgothal and render aid as needed. Not long after, we made ready a company of Argain Dragons and dove from the sky. And once landed, the group commander then gave the message of the fallen Hymmnaught of Growgothal."

Vessiel looked to Corian, listening. "Mighty Pirah had left Avalon to render aid to one stricken of Argain who had been bitten several times by the half-serpent Zu and were in danger of passing. This Dragon was of high placing in the court of Serous Drakkus and very dear to him as well, and haste was of utmost importance. The Lady Rhona could not see the added time it would take to fly the physicians and so bid the remaining Mystics to break the spell that prevented the portaling, and so Lord Quainor made the attempt again and again until exhausted. Many others tried and tried until one who was a prisoner, a Mystic assassin that had been sent by the accursed to kill Lord Pirah and failed, came forth and bid that he should try. For apparently, he was no longer in the favor of Favlos and would prove himself useful to the enemies of his former master. He did conjure but not as the mystics before him. He bid that Lord Quainor open the portal at Avalon only and maintain the opening.

"As this was done, the prisoner turned ally summoned a great apparition that was controlled by his own movements, and thus did he place a great hammer into the hands of the massive construct and directed it to swing it at the opening created by Lord Quainor. A great and deafening crash resounded, shaking the very fabric of the Mystic realm! Again and again, he did make the apparition smash his hammer until there was a distortion in the air, and again did he bring forth the onslaught until what was witnessed by your own troops the shattering of the Mystic fabric and the arrival of the Centaur host. Your Grace."

Corian then bowed and stepped away, leaving Vessiel to her thoughts and the grief that set in well before the passing of her husband and King. She stood there in the hall for quite some time, her attendants and personal guard waiting just out of view but well within earshot. She then strode down the hallway, her guards and attendants falling into step behind her. She followed the hallways until ending at a great arched entryway that took her out to a large outdoor palisade that she crossed, with the entourage just behind her.

Once across the palisade, the Queen of Ogres entered another arched entryway and yet another long hallway that led to a doorway of a sacred room where only she may enter. The entourage came to a sharp halt and took up positions about the hall to ensure that the Queen would not be disturbed. The attendant within the room closed the great double doors, and the Queen locked them behind her then turned to the full-sized stone carving of what would be called and revered as the father of Ogres from the first age of the gathering of Ogres many ages past. Vessiel lowered herself to her knees and then bent forward, placed her hands to the floor, and lowered her head until it, too, touched the floor in the ultimate show of reverence to the image that was the for-bearer of her now late husband and King. Aufneunec's name lived in the heart of all Ogres of the Mystic realm. Though he was not a God, his part in the creation of the realm of Ogres and bringing about of the manifestation of Growgothal placed him as close to divine as any Ogre could become.

Vessiel raised her head and sat back on her heels, placing her hands on her thighs as she faced the statue of Aufneunec and began to address the Father of Ogres. "Father of us all, I beg you harken to my voice for I am to commit a great defiance of my beloved Hymmnaught's last wishes, and I would bare my intentions to you. Loe, did my King, with his last breath, speak his love for me, his Wife and Queen, and for the secession of the throne of Growgothal and to pledge fealty to those that would go to war with the accursed and those that have joined him in his madness."

She stopped for a moment, knowing she was going to follow through with a grave action that bordered on treason even for a Queen. "I will see to it that one of our sons doth take the throne through the ancient ways of trial by combat, but I will not rest until the Half Giant Bastards of Celoth are erased from the Mystic Realm and wherever they may find refuge. I will unleash the armies of Growgothal and decimate them until they are no more, with axe, sword, and spear, and hammer, with Magic that conjures hideous apparitions and beyond. I swear to the last Ogre, if it be me, then let it be so. I will avenge my beloved Hymmnaught, and only then will I ally my armies to the rest. I commit myself to this. I ask for no forgiveness. I am an Ogre."

She then put her head to the floor once again and rose to her feet, straitened her garments, walked to the doors of the chamber, and unlocked them. As she left the chamber, her entourage snapped to attention. An attendant approached and bowed to Vessiel. "The pyre for His Highness is ready, my Queen. We are transporting his body to the site as we speak," the attendant said.

"Very well, then let us send our King to the next world, for there are tidings waiting for Hymmnaught."

The procession was long, and moved slowly the numbers of Ogres, swelling to the point of the road being overwhelmed and mourners pouring out over the fields as they approached the raised mound of earth where atop was the scaffold that was to be Hymmnaught's last place of rest before his body was set ablaze and his spirit cold then move on. Six very large Ogres carried his body on a stretcher made of axe and spear shafts, as was the custom when bringing an Ogre that died in combat to its funeral pyre. Clutched in the hands of their King was his favorite war axe. His armor had been polished, and his tusks had been equipped with sharpened steel points, for he might have need of his weapons if the Greater Powers see fit to cast him elsewhere.

There were many pyres about, for there were many that had died in the battle for the capital, but none stood as high as Hymmnaught. The throngs that gathered had begun to sing in low tones an ancient dirge that had been passed down by so many generations that spanned the existence of the Ogres since the first age. As the bearers of Hymmnaught's body climbed the mound, his right leg slipped from the stretcher, causing many to react as if Hymmnaught were awakening, and before any could think twice of the incident, a voice in Ogre roared, "Even now mighty Hymmnaught will not give in to death!" This brought out huge roars of laughter and undying loyalty to their King now past.

His leg was righted on the stretcher, and his body placed upon the scaffolding and those close to him brought forth gifts of strong brew and personal weapons, articles of clothing, and gold, that he might have treasures to barter with should he need them. So many were the gifts that they began to cover the mound. Such beloved friends did the King of Ogres have. When the last gift was laid upon the heap the crowd did part and noble Vessiel came forward with a lit torch, and as she turned to speak to the throngs of her Husband and King, the Generals of Growgothal poured oil about the mound and scaffold so that all the gifts would burn with Hymmnaught so as to make the journey with him to the next world. All became silent as Vessiel, the Queen of Ogres, began to speak.

"My subjects, my people, Ogres, you have all gathered here to pay homage to great Hymmnaught, our King, the father of my children, and my one truly beloved. Others would grieve the death of their King and be sorrowful, but that is not our way, and Mighty Hymmnaught would have none of it. He would have us feast and carry on and make merry, for his death was a grand death. The count of those slain by his hand, those that felt the kiss of his axe and the cut of his blade, still goes on. The tally will be heavy indeed, my brothers and sisters. The ground where he stood still runs with the blood of our enemies, those foolhardy enough to be within his reach."

Vessiel paused but for a moment. "His Majesty Hymmnaught the Ogre would have us all drink and gorge and fornicate until we exhaust all that we could muster in his name, for we are Ogres. Say goodbye, my people, before I cast this torch upon the mound and light the pyre of our King, my beloved, the greatest of Ogres."

Vessiel then turned and thrust the torch on to the mound that was covered in gifts and watched as the oil that had been spread about the pyre ignited, trailing all around the gifts placed about the mound. The flames slithered up to the scaffold where Hymmnaught's body lay, and as it was touched by the flames, it virtually erupted in a fiery ball that formed a mushroom in the sky, lighting up the countryside for a great distance. Vessiel looked to the night sky, transfixed on the fireball that was once her beloved, and all those around did the same until she lowered her head and slowly turned. She then, with a very slow gait, began to leave the scene of the pyre, her twenty-four offspring lining up in twos behind her. As she walked, the high General of Growgothal's armies joined her, keeping pace with the Queen. She motioned that he come closer so as not to let anyone near them hear what she was about to tell him.

"General," She started. General Tarlus, who had fought side by side with Hymmnaught, had also sustained injuries that had been stitched with hide and twine after being cauterized to stop the bleeding. Though they looked very painful, one would not know by his demeanor.

He tilted his head to acknowledge he understood her meaning of discretion. Vessiel continued. "I have a mission for you and the rest of the commanders of my armies, one that will set aside the orders of my late beloved. Do you understand?"

Tarlus looked at his queen for a moment as they walked and then answered, "I do, Your Grace."

She continued. "You will gather the armies to full strength, acquire all of the resources needed, mercenaries if you must, make plans, and gather intelligence to annihilate the Celoth completely from the Mystic Realm."

Tarlus's facial expression did not change as Vessiel gave him his task. He simply replied, "Revenge, my queen?"

"Yes," Said Vessiel.

"It shall be done, for it is the wish of my Queen."

Tarlus bowed and turned away from the procession with his personal guard and the command generals of Growgothal. His next in command picked up his pace, took up next to him, and inquired, "Orders, my Lord General?"

Tarlus had a scowl across his mouth that was the Ogre version of a grin, and without turning, he replied, "Gather the Armies, my Lord, the entirety of them. We have a task."

CHAPTER 2

Zu: Villain, Vile, Victor

Favlos lay in his great bed, smelling of ale, wine, and smoking intoxicants mixed with traces of sex, having enjoyed a long bout of debauchery for the last several days. This was how he had spent his time, waiting for news of the exploits of his servant Lords that were unleashed upon the Mystic Realm. He enjoyed having carnal pleasure with different races and species, including humans and human-like forms of life, and found it much more enjoyable with actual beings as opposed to constructs that he could create with little effort. He had not fully woken yet as he drifted back and forth into sleep until he had opened his eyes to the sunlight becoming ever brighter through the great doorways from the balcony of his large bedchamber.

He let the haze leave his eyes before looking about at the disheveled appearance of the room. There were several male and female humans and fairies lying about, still unconscious from the revelry and near perpetual sex put upon them by their host or captor depending on the individual case, that is. Favlos found himself enjoying the males that had been absconded with from the Mortal realm as some of them actually enjoyed themselves as though they were having some sort of dream that is, until he had them taken to the Trolls for their various uses, which ordinarily ended with them being eaten. The Centauress he had chained to the floor was wide awake; she was yet to be had and with good reason, she having killed just about everyone who came close to her. Favlos decided he would seduce her with spells that evening and share her with the Celoth Lord if he would so indulge.

Having come to complete awareness of his state of being, Favlos could feel just the hint detoxification in progress that would ensue in a monumental hangover, and the hair of the dog would be necessary in the immediate sense. While gazing about the room, he could feel something moving about in his bed, slithering up to the region of his loins, the touch of fingers tracing their way up his thighs and taking hold of his flaccid cock. This would-be sexual purveyor began to caress and stroke the ever-growing organ until it reached an impressive state of tumescent rigidity. The hidden bed companion continued to fondle his loins as Favlos pulled the bedclothes from over the head of Lady Algala.

"Good morning, my lady," Said the Accursed as she brushed her long dark tresses away. She made a hand gesture to a washcloth and a bowl of water that sat on a small table, using magic to bring them to her she, then snatched the cloth from the air, dunked it into the bowl that hung in midair, wrung out the excess water, and released it, sending it forward to wrap around the still-erect cock of Favlos. Using hand manipulations, she washed it and then sent the cloth and bowl back to where they had rest before as she once again took hold of his now clean sex with a regard that could only be called fixation.

Lady Algala spoke. "I prefer a clean cock in my mouth, Holiness, especially since your cock has been in every ass and pussy in this room but for the half nag in the corner. Saving her for later?" She didn't miss a beat as she opened her mouth ever wider than a woman should be able to and, with a sucking sound, engulfed his cock halfway down the shaft. Favlos let out a half-grunting and half-moaning sound as Lady Algala worked her oral mastery, bobbing and sucking while occasionally licking his shaft and testicles.

With the worst timing in the world, there was a knocking at the door to Favlos's chambers. Algala did not stop as Favlos tried to hold back the ever-building climax. The knocking was again heard, and Favlos could not contain himself a moment longer, the sensation causing his already throbbing cock to grow in her throat to the point where she could not have it so without strangling herself. She sucked the head and stroked his shaft with one hand and caressed his balls with the other until he burst in her mouth in pulsing gushes that filled it much too quickly for her to swallow. She pulled his erupting member from her mouth and stroked it ever purposefully so as to paint her breasts with his ejaculations, her protruding porcelain mounds highlighted by colorful seafaring tattoos. Once again the knocking came, only much louder and with urgency. Favlos didn't even try to contain his vocalization at his explosive climax, bellowing loud enough to wake everyone in the room and giving those outside the door reason to believe there might be foul play in their ruler's chamber. They burst through the door.

Four of the palace guards and two of the court of Favlos charged into the room, swords drawn and plasma flames undulating in the palms of the courtiers. To the embarrassed looks of the would-be rescuers, there came the chuckling of Lady Algala and the huffing and sighing of their King, Favlos, as well as the giggling of the other occupants of the room, save the Centauress, who had an angry scowl on her face. With a powerful jerk, she snapped taut the chain that was secured around her human waist and restraining her arms at the wrist. The six barged in at the inopportune moment, and as one dropped to one knee, daring not to look up and meet the eye of their Lord and master. Algala wiped her mouth off but did little to clean the rest of her work from her as she reveled in her audacity as much as being lewd.

Favlos regained his composure enough to pour himself some wine from across the room and motion it to him. As he caught the goblet, he nodded to the six men kneeling before him, and as one they stood. The others that had been part of Favlos's entertainment gathered pieces of clothing and other garments, covering themselves and pouring their own goblets to fend off the ailments of post debauchery consumption.

At that moment, yet another figure entered the room and took his place in the formation of those that serve the Dark Lord. Favlos took yet another long draft of wine and addressed the seventh form. "Lord Turkez Loque, how fair you this grand day?"

"Quite well, Holiness, for I bring tidings of victory in the campaign of continuing engagement and withdrawal. The attack on the Ogre realm brought unforeseen bounty and one achievement that could be seen as nothing more than a stroke of luck. You see, His Majesty Hymmnaught, King of Growgothal, has fallen."

Favlos sat for a moment, considering what he had just heard, thinking of what could be happening in the Mystic realm as the word spread that the beloved of his enemies, Hymmnaught, met his demise. As he pondered this, Lady Algala rose from his bed clothed in only her tattoos and a few pieces of jewelry. She bore no modesty and still showed the glistening aftermath of her previous servicing of the King of Corsolvess. She walked slowly over to the same washbasin, picked up a dry cloth, moistened it, then slowly wiped the streaks and droplets from her breasts while the others from the court stole glances of her. She met each glance with come-hither looks. Each man knew that if he were to give the merest notion of a response, the penalty would be severe.

All, save who Turkez, looked directly at her with little or no emotion save the arching of his left eyebrow, expressing his lack of interest. This did not deter the comely Algala in her personal desire for lusty attention, for there were others in the room to play with. Favlos looked directly at Turkez, having thought about what was just divulged, and asked, "You are certain of this, my Lord Turkez? There is no mistake?"

"None, Holiness, the King of Ogres met his demise after slaying a great number of Celoth and being pierced time and time again with arrows until finally struck with a Dragon lance, and even then, not right away did he fall until the egress was sound. Yet he did pass in his chamber, and a funeral was held, Holiness," Turkez replied.

"Has a successor been named?"

"Not as yet, Holiness. It seems the Ogre Queen has other plans not yet exposed to me. However, Lord Zu has had much success on his end in creating havoc in the Dragon Realm, Argain, and of course, Eschrokahn Veh. Was this the task that Holiness bid him perform?"

"Indeed it was, my Lord. Indeed, it shall continue."

Favlos turned his gaze to the guests that had been sharing the festivities where Lady Algala was tending to her wants with two males from Corsolvess and one female Brownie (one can never be sure of the sex of a Brownie without investigation), then turned back to Turkez and company. "Now, my lord, unless you are going to join us and the she pirate, I bid you and company good morrow." Turkez bowed and turned around, leaving the room with the previous six following behind him, the last stopping to close the door and get one last glance at the debauchery once again in session.

"It is good that His Holiness is pleased with the tidings brought this morning, yes?" one of the courtiers asked of Turkez as they proceeded down the hall.

"Only for now I'm sure, for the king has many such desires to be fulfilled. Let us hope that his current distraction keeps him happy for the sake of all our lives," Turkez replied. The group continued in silence to their respective chambers, and the guards proceeded to the great hall of the king.

Turkez continued to the great chamber of lords, where the generals and admirals of Favlos's forces congregated and made plans for the upcoming actions and raids to be conducted in the name of their king. When he entered the room, he noticed the ever-present multilimbed General Wormskale and several of his subordinates of the same species, speaking in hushed tones until one of the group noticed Turkez. Made all aware, they gave a curt bow to the high counsel of Corsolvess, then continued their conversation. He also noticed the ever-conspicuous absence of Admiral Quinstems. Although this was nothing new, Turkez could not help but have a feeling of distrust for the admiral at this particular juncture.

Though there was no place of stature in this room, it was plain that Turkez was the highest of station within its walls, and all paid deference to him as he walked to a table that had been covered with food and several vessels of ales and wine. One of the servants poured him a cup, and as he took it, a voice came from behind him. "I trust our King is in good spirits this morning, my lord Turkez?" The high council turned to see Admiral Quinstems standing before him, appearing almost out of thin air. Turkez waited until he could absorb the expression on the face of the elusive admiral, which was never an easy thing, even for one as adept as he. Quinstems, being of a multi-appendaged species, that came about during the first age of man on Earth Mother, originated on an island continent that would be located closest to the area that would be called the Gulf of Arabia or thereabouts. Earth Mother having shifted the surface several times had changed the geography.

Limbed Alnnas Mutaeaddida was the name given to his kind by the men of that age, meaning "multilimbed people." Their large stature and immortality gave them deity status for the times. The name they would use for themselves was Gegen. The forebears of Favlos saw them as a unique resource and wasted no time corrupting them to their ways. However, in every such scenario, there was always the unexpected faction that may have other ideas. Turkez, after his appraising pause, finally answered.

"Indeed, my Lord Admiral. Holiness was definitely pleased with the results of the assault on the capital of Growgothal and entirely pleased with Lord Zu having ravaged the Argain, the keep of Drakkus, not to mention the personal escort of the King of Dragons is mortally injected, after which he took his small host and slaughtered every living thing in the rookeries of Eschrokahn Veh. Well, I suppose the unhatched and newly hatched that he consumed lived for a time longer, but not much." A strange leer crossed the lips of Admiral Quinstems. as he took a draft from his own goblet of ale, he also took a piece of beef with his upper right hand from a plate he held with his middle left hand (He had no lower left hand) and ripped it apart with his middle and upper right hands then filled his mouth with the sumptuous meat.

"What know you of any activities our Lord General Wormskale has in progress,, my lord?" asked Turkez of Quinstems.

"I really can't say. One could conjecture from his past attempts that he is planning an attack that seems most devastating to our enemies, only to have the tides turned and his forces all but annihilated, or he has something of a covert nature that we don't give him any due credit for, having the intellect to conceive my Lord council." All the while chewing as he spoke, Quinstems then took another draft of ale. "I believe His Holiness will be celebrating Lord Zu this day once he has had his fill of recreation." Turkez continued. "Much to the disappointment of Wormskale, perhaps yourself as well, my Lord Admiral?"

Quinstems dabbed his mouth with a hand towel, taking advantage of a pregnant pause, then spoke matter-of-factually. "For myself, not in the least, but I shall not speak for my landlocked counterpart. You see, with this altered way of engagement that we have been employing, the fluidity of combat has become quite fluid if you get my meaning."

Turkez sipped at his wine and ran his fingers over his long white beard while looking about for anyone who may have been listening then replied. "I believe I do, Lord Admiral." They both exchanged curt bows and parted company for the time being; Quinstems mingled a bit and then disappeared within the very room itself while Turkez took a seat and was soon surrounded by those of an ingratiating nature. The members of Favlos's court and his advisers engaged Turkez in seemingly meaningless conversation, all the while trying to glean what information they could about current possibilities of the termination of higher lords or the successes that may have occurred.

While all this was going on, the doors of the room were opened, and a herald announced that Lord Zu has arrived. The room went silent as the herald continued by informing the high lords of Corsolvess to make ready for festivities in Lord Zu's honor that evening. General Wormskale was not pleased in the slightest and did not conceal his feelings as his face grimaced.

He turned to his subordinates. "Come. Let us celebrate the snake that kisses the ass of our king." Wormskale turned and walked from the room. As his commanders fell into step behind him, he motioned for his master of spies to come to his side. General Arteous picked up his pace to see to his Lord General's beckoning. As he approached, Wormskale spoke in low tones. "Are you quite certain of this intelligence from Avalon?"

"Without question, my Lord, I have seen the very description I gave you through the eyes of the parasitic placed within the ranks of the Avalon Guardians by means of poisoning one of them which we came upon at a brothel," Arteous replied.

"Excellent. Let us place our options into action as I present these tidings to Our Holiness".

"Assassinate the assassin, my lord?"

"Unless you can bring him in alive, my lord general."

"Why cause such undue ruckus when a corpse is so much more compliant, my lord?" Arteous replied. The group proceeded to their own quarters in the castle of the king to make ready for the celebration of Lord Zu's accomplishments. The rest of the occupants of the assembly room also made their way out to prepare for the oncoming event. Wormskale was not the only high lord in Favlos's command structure with resentment toward Lord Zu; all for the sake of their positions and very survival, he also had to play this game of placating and defamation.

Favlos seemed to enjoy watching his generals, advisers, and courtiers possessing magical abilities shifting their positions like game pieces on a board to curry favor from one high lord to the next, with the ultimate goal of becoming closest to him. His vanity knew no bounds, as well as his lust and desire for ultimate deified control over Mystic and Mortal realms, and those that served him with the most zeal would be highest in his favor. Wormskale had his own ideas for certain; he knew he had fallen from his previous stature and needed to leap over Quinstems—and perhaps Zu.

The evening came, and the throne room filled with those that gave council and other needs to the God king Favlos as well as copious numbers of other attendees with the sole purpose of pleasure for all those present. As the celebration progressed and the guests became more festive, there were conversations regarding what outcome was the conflict to bring and where each of them might find themselves. The speculation and predetermined assumptions flew here and there, all with no real substance, only with the purpose of redirecting one or all from their own agenda. Yet each knew that the slightest mistake in the game that was constantly being played could spell absolute ruin, expulsion, and of course, a very painful death by the whim of the king. So play this game they did, all with their own skill and tenacity for the acquisition of what table scrap they might receive.

The moment of the arrival of the king and his serpent lord had come, and all were called to attention by Lord Turkez.

"All hail His Holiness, King Favlos, lord of Corsolvess and ruler of the Mystic realm and all those beyond."

The occupants of the great throne room dropped to one knee but for those encumbered by species and as one recited, "That which is mine is yours, Holiness." Favlos once again appeared from the back of the massive Dragon's skull that made his throne and took his seat in its mouth as a servant maid brought him a goblet of wine. "Will you join us my Lord?" said Favlos without looking any particular direction. He then commanded that all rise to show homage to the guest of honor.

There was a sound of something being dragged across wooden beams that came from the high ceiling, where no light reached, then in an instant, a huge pair of red eyes appeared, as if emitting their own light source. The eyes became a face that had the look of a Dragon yet the features of a serpent, and as the eyes became visible, the light became also serpent-like, with multifaceted irises and almost undetectable pupils. As the head dropped down, so did several coils and lengths from other areas of the ceiling, which gave all a feeling of foreboding at the discovery of Zu having been lying in silence in the rafters as they had conversed before the entrance of Favlos. Those of lesser powers and stature made themselves less visible, knowing Zu's penchant for killing for pleasure those that have little or no way to defend themselves and, if not killing, frightening them to the point of humiliation. The others regarded Zu as the one closest to Favlos and, if given the opportunity, would remove him altogether, which would make the game that much more provocative. But alas, the lifelong friend of the King enjoyed his own power and prestige, and the removal process would be somewhat complicated for those with little knowledge of planning and executing. For this, the field of play for those endeavors was quite small.

Zu brought his entire length down from the shadows of the rafters and made a circle of his body around the throne, a symbolic movement to both the King and those of the court to see with whom his highest loyalties lay and that he was both protected and protector. In this gesture alone, he had shown that any attempts to put him in disfavor would be squashed without consideration. The attendees lavished Lord Zu with long-lasting applause and congratulations for his victories and accomplishments. The lower the member of Favlos's court, the more enthusiastic the praise, for they knew above all that it would be one or more of them that could find themselves in Zu's interest or his coils. The applause continued for a time until Favlos waved his hand for silence; he then addressed the room.

"Behold, my loyal servants and those that serve them. Our lord Zu has returned from tasks that I bid him take, and with his skills and guile, he did strike a hurtful blow to our enemies." There was a short pause, then he began again. "Fear now resides in the hearts of Dragons and men of the Mystic realm, and that shall be the common thread among them from now on. And those of my forces that bring about the most fear to our foes shall find themselves richly rewarded. Let this be the endeavor of you all. So now let us feast and drink and celebrate our Lord Zu." The room let out a cheer, raised their cups and flagons to Lord Zu, and then proceeded to fill their plates and converse among themselves. And though the mood seemed festive, there was still the underlying current of fear that something may occur that evening that would involve the bloodshed of one or more of the attendees for the sport of it or perhaps just as a reminder of how quickly the mood of Favlos could change. Most of Favlos's retainers and allies were present, except for the one that would be the most obvious next to Zu, and that was the Celoth Lord Orokoth, whose mere proportions would have made him the center of attention, followed by Amirchesch, the Lord of the Borian Dragon riders. These two arguably were the most powerful of his collective. Lady Algala chose not to accompany Favlos as she would not be claimed as anyone's prize, whether man, Lord, or King; that would be too constricting for one such as her of many tastes.

Neither of the two lords had portal to the keep of Favlos yet, for they had plans to conceive and put into action in the name of the King. The celebration turned to great revelry and laughter. Women were dashing about with pitchers of ale and flagons of wine to keep every cup and chalice full. There were servants with great trays on their shoulders, heavily laden with meat and vegetables, to fill the plates of guests without need of them moving from their seats. Minstrels played soft tones at first then picked up the tempo for the barely clad dancing girls that performed for the crowd, stirring all with ideas lustful play.

Favlos stayed at his throne, not having any real desire to mingle with those of his court; however, he did enjoy gazing about the room and watching as the people themselves interacted and played their game of politics with bribes and corrosion and, of course, the promise of once-denied sex. This sort of thing to the king of Corsolvess was like taking in a performance, only having the edge of real life. His viewing pleasure was interrupted by the familiar voice of the guest of honor, whose head dropped down in front of him from the top of his Dragon's skull throne adornment. "Must I stay for the entire festivities? I do have other wonderful ideas to make into reality."

"It would be somewhat of a useless celebration if the reason for celebrating is not at the celebration, my Lord," Answered Favlos. Zu bowed and retracted his head for the skull then uncoiled himself from around the throne and redistributed himself about the stairs that extended to the left and right of the throne apron. As he moved, he kept his head stationary so as to watch the crowd and perhaps single out an interesting morsel, but only for sport, for his stomach had not yet finished with the Eschrokahn Veh he had gorged himself on. All did their best not to meet with the gaze of Zu, for that would most likely invite calamity.

There were, however, those who did not fear the serpent, having their own means to dispatch those that would give them cause, one of those being Turkez and several other members of Favlos's court. These were the individuals that gave Zu only required deference due to his status with the King. Not to be denied his infamy, Admiral Quinstems did appear from behind a pillar and very deftly made his way to the throne apron and to the very face of Zu. The half-serpent grinned and spoke. "Someday you must share your secrets with me, Lord Admiral."

"What secret would that be, my Lord?" He replied.

"The ability to appear as if out of nowhere, anywhere." Zu elevated his head so as to look down on Quinstems, giving him a stance of superiority, although much to his dismay, it had no effect on the Admiral.

"Ah, well, it's quite simple actually. You simply be where you are not seen until you wish to be seen, my lord." Zu would not show if he was annoyed even if he was but did tilt his head slightly as he regarded Quinstems.

"How very interesting, my Lord. Such simplicity would elude even the most brilliant, definitely." Quinstems grinned and took a large swallow from his cup.

"I would imagine any smaller application of intellect would expose your technique, Admiral. Do be vigilant."

"I shall, as always, Lord Zu. It is what I do, in the service of His Holiness." Quinstems bowed, placing one hand over his breastplate while taking a step back, never taking his eyes off Zu. This exchange did not go unnoticed by Wormskale and the other lords of the court, and the speculation nearly whipped up frenzy in the great hall, the question being what was discussed with Zu and Quinstems, and once again, where Quinstems came from. Those that wanted to pry out these answers were greatly disappointed, as once again, the high lord admiral vanished from sight, and engaging Zu would be tantamount to suicide. Wormskale wanted to present his new findings to his king at the right moment; however, that moment had yet to arrive. As the celebration went on, others did find liquid courage to approach Zu, only to give praise to the favorite of the king, minding not to take too much of his time, lest they be thought an "interesting diversion" to the half serpent.

As luck would have it for the guests and servants, Zu was not interested in terrifying or consuming any of them; he had other ideas to give him pleasure, and that had to do with raiding and creating mayhem. It seemed that the tasks he was sent to do reignited his joy for destruction and murder, and he wanted more of it. Lolling about with these ingratiating rodents was only boring him to death. But much to his chagrin, a line began to form after the celebrants had noticed that approaching Zu had not caused any ill effects, so they set about showing deference to the guest of honor in acknowledgment of his deeds. Zu decided he would allow this for His Holiness's sake and managed not to frighten anyone too much for the next hour or so.

Wormskale kept from engaging with Zu for the most part. There was never any real acknowledgment between the two, each considering the other as something that had to be tolerated, for each had his place in the king's dynamic. The general found his moment to approach Favlos with the acquired intelligence that would change his standing. While those that would ingratiate themselves with Zu, Wormskale approached the Dragon's skull and dropped to one knee, with one hand at his breastplate and the rest spread wide. Favlos acknowledged his high general.

"Good day, my lord general."

"And to you, Holiness. May I approach and speak to you?"

"What do you have for us, General?" he asked.

"A small, yet interesting parcel that may bring enlightenment to you, Holiness."

"Come forward, General. You have intrigued us." Wormskale rose and walked between the mandibles of the Dragon's skull; he bowed once again as Favlos regarded him with a peculiar curiosity.

"I have for you, Holiness, the answer to your query, and I believe this intelligence to be accurate."

"Do you, my lord?" replied Favlos.

"I do." Wormskale reached into his tunic, produced a rolled parchment, and handed it to Favlos, who opened it with a skeptical look on his face. This look changed as he read what Wormskale called "enlightening."

After finishing the note, he looked up at his high general and asked, "You have contingencies in place?"

"Contingencies in progress, Holiness." Favlos stared out at the crowd yet saw no one, for he was in thought and anger simultaneously and was restraining himself from going on a heinous tirade from what he had discovered but a second ago. Yet he then found himself calmed. "If possible, bring me his traitorous head," said the accursed.

"Well done, Lord General." Wormskale bowed once again and turned. Knowing his audience with the king was concluded and he had more than the desired effect, he could barely conceal his self-satisfied smirk as he walked from the skull throne and was then joined by his subordinates.

General Arteous approached and spoke. "Orders, my lord general?"

"Yes, instruct those you have placed in Avalon to bring the head of my lord Feckulis to me, and make haste." Arteous bowed and left with his aides following behind him. Wormskale made his way to a pile of soft cushions and lay down with a very indulgent grin on his face while considering the comely serving girl that filled his chalice, all the while being observed by the steely eyes of Turkez and others of the court, each pondering what was in the note he handed to their king. Zu had reached the zenith of his tolerance for the ingratiating crowed that had formed around him and decided it was time to retreat or do something either horrifying or at least terribly rude.

"My lords and ladies, I must take my leave, for all of this celebration has taken its toll upon me. But please do enjoy what His Holiness has provided." Zu then slithered across the throne room floor to the Dragon skull and wrapped his front portion around it to bring his head to the same level as the accursed, who greeted him with a smirk.

"Had quite enough, my friend?" asked Favlos.

Zu gave a long glance toward the celebrants and replied, "That, my king, is an overstatement. I had had enough before this gathering began. I go to plot my next artistic campaign, in His Holiness's service." Zu bowed as Favlos did in return; he then coiled around one of the great pillars in the throne room and made his way back to the shadows of the high ceiling, where he slithered through one of his many passageways that led to his quarters. Favlos sat in contemplation of what he had read on the note from General Wormskale, mulling not so much on the betrayal of his mercenary assassin but perhaps some others as well. He would consult with Turkez.

The revelers continued their festive goings-on some losing all inhibition, as this happened quite a bit at these occasions, and comely servants, both male and female, became objects of lustful need. Victorious celebration became an orgy for the sexually engrossed and visual stimulus for the voyeuristically disposed. Favlos gazed about. Seeing this reminded him that he had a guest still chained to the floor in his bedchamber, and he decided that he would not share this one but would have his way with her himself. He took yet another long draft from his goblet, then a serving maid filled it for him. As she did, Favlos examined her full breasts that were unfettered beneath her shirt and decided yet again, perhaps an appetizer before the main course. The comely wench did smile at her king's attention. Favlos leered back.

CHAPTER 3

Pirah

Lady Aralainious lay quietly on massive cushions, her wings folded onto her back while her ever-long neck and tail coiled about her body. She was at rest and breathing rhythmically, at long last after having been bitten many times by the most fowl Zu and having been injected with his serpent's venom while being held by giants. Normally, such odds would give her little challenge, but Zu only needed the momentary distraction to sink his fangs into Aralainious's flesh, where the scales were not—these places being the wing shoulder joint and areas under the arms. Her wounds were all but healed and the poison had been extracted, and now it was time for her to recover. For the venom of Zu did take its toll—not enough, however, for the abilities of an Argain to regenerate while at rest.

Lord Pirah and Lady Badi Ah Azizah stood close to Aralainious, making sure she was entirely without complication before leaving her to her healing process and returning to Avalon—and the fight to come. Badi Ah reached out and touched Aralainious just under her eye in a gesture of compassion, and as she did, the great eye opened and focused for a second on the tall Elf and then slowly closed, with a slight twitch of the corner of her mouth—a Dragon's version of smile. Pirah took Badi Ah by the hand, and they both stepped away to leave her in peace. As they walked through the halls of healing in the great Argain castle that was the keep of Drakkus, Badi Ah spoke to Pirah in hushed tones, for the size of the halls and passageways of this place were immense and caused echoes everlasting, and she did not want to disturb those at rest. "My lord, will Lady Aralainious be made whole again?"

"Yes, child, but not without some scarring. But not to worry for she has fought many battles and is not without those scars. Aralainious is truly a Warrior and, of course, Argain. So worry not. I have removed the venom from her being, and now it is time for her to heal. Let us get back to Avalon to deal with what other damage has been done."

Pirah and Badi Ah continued down the hallway until they came to the courtyard, where Kelos Voc and ten fully armed Argain Dragons were in conversation. As Pirah approached, General Voc spoke. "How does my lady fare, my lord?"

"She will recover, Lord General. Of that I am certain. However, I believe there should be more guards set in place for her and all about Argain, and the keep of Drakkus more so. This tactic of the accursed seems to have no rhyme or reason, and he knows no bounds"

"An excellent thought, my lord. I shall make it so at once." Kelos Voc looked to his group of officers who were listening to the exchange and made a gesture, and as one they all bowed and took flight with one stroke of their wings.

Kelos Voc then asked, "What is next, my lord? Do you have word from His Royal Majesty?"

"None as of yet, Lord General. However, I am sure that the armies of Argain shall assemble at full strength along with Eschrokahn Veh and the others," answered Pirah.

"I shall put the assembly in motion, my lord, and await the call of King Drakkus." Kelos Voc then took flight and was gone in an instant. Pirah then addressed Badi Ah.

"We must go now and see to Avalon and all those that would banner with her."

"My heart burns for the fray, my lord. Let us hasten," Badi Ah replied.

"Your heart will be quenched, my love, a hundredfold times a hundred, I'm sure."

Pirah made a hand motion of his own, opening a portal in the fabric of the Mystic realm that would take them to Avalon, where the armies—or at the very least, emissaries pledging loyalty in the coming struggle—were no doubt assembling. Pirah knew that this would not be contained in the realm of mystical beings; he knew that this was headed into the world of Mortals and most of the battles would be fought on the face of Earth Mother, and life, once again, would never be the same.

Etilgam Inim stood before the portal that had opened in the courtyard, just at the bottom steps that sat at the base of the palisade before the great hall of Avalon, knowing who was about to emerge from it and bracing himself for the impassioned greeting of his beloved pupil Badi Ah Aziza and then the news from Lord Pirah about the condition of Lady Aralainious. As soon as the portal completed, out stepped Badi Ah Aziza, whose first sight was her teacher and name giver. So without hesitation, she scooped him up in her loving arms and nearly crushed him between her breasts, showering his face and head with kisses. She then released him, showing no shame for her display of affection, and then simply addressed him. "My lord, it is wonderful to see you."

"Now, child, it has only been a few weeks. Let us not become overzealous," Etilgam said.

"I shall if I wish," she answered as she bent over and grabbed a handful of beard and pulled his mouth to hers for one more kiss. Though they had not become physical, there was no doubt that Badi Ah had a deep love for Lord Inim as he was instrumental in her transformation and education in the ways of Avalon and the Mystic realm. As for Etilgam Inim, he had fought from the moment she had been remade the urge to take her, for she had great sexual attraction with her beauty and stature—this, combined with the manner of dress she chose when not in armor, preferring to expose her endless limbs and full hips with light clothes and silks, as well as plunging necklines.

However, at this time, she was adorned in the light armor of an archer, for that was the skill she had gravitated to, as well as the two short swords of the design that came from Earth Mother in the land of Nippon (Wasakashi). The keepers of the archives of humans' history compiled a long and comprehensive inventory of swords and other cutting weapons from every age that had been given life and had developed on her surface, and Badi Ah had wanted to learn them all. She then walked from the site as Etilgam and Pirah conversed about the goings-on for the last few weeks since the attack on Growgothal and Argain as well as the arrival of Eschrokahn Veh to the fold.

"What of Growgothal and beloved Hymmnaught, my lord Etilgam? Did the Centaur host arrive in time?" Pirah asked.

"I'm afraid not, my lord. Apparently, Corian and the physicians that went with him arrived seconds too late to save the king. He is fallen."

"You are saying Hymmnaught?" Pirah said, almost shouting in disbelief.

"Aye, my lord, King Hymmnaught has passed from wounds suffered at the very gates of the capital of Growgothal, fighting the Celoth hoard no doubt sent by the accursed with the Borians attacking from the sky." Pirah stood feeling shock and disbelief over the news of his dear, beloved Hymmnaught, whom he had visited only some months ago and had known for so very, very long. The shock became anger, with the desire to reap vengeance for his friend upon all those that had anything to do with his death, but then Vessiel came to mind as well as the twenty-four children of Hymmnaught. Sadness then came over mighty Pirah that there would be more to come, much more.

"What of Vessiel, my lord? Has there been any word from the queen?" Etilgam answered.

"None, my lord, only that the armies of Growgothal are forming for battle, yet there have been no heralds or messages of any sort." Pirah thought for a moment then motioned Etilgam to walk with him as they headed into the great hall of Avalon. As they walked, Pirah went over the events of the last months that passed since the attack on Avalon as well as Growgothal and the Dragon realm, Argain, putting together the pieces of what he suspected were the true purpose of these attacks without meaning, yet he could not see just what the true end this chaos was to bring. He addressed Etilgam.

"What of the successor to Growgothal's thrown? Has Vessiel begun the trials?"

"Not as yet, my lord." Pirah continued to the great hall, where the keepers had already been wakened, and the massive stone doors had been opened. Pirah looked about the doors and the keepers and said to Etilgam, "Perhaps the keepers should be left awakened in these dark times, my lord, for who knows when we may expect an attack?"

"It has been done, my lord Pirah," Etilgam answered with a grin. The two of them continued through the great doorway as the keepers placed their axes to their chest in salute. Upon entering the passageway to the hall of Avalon, Pirah noticed that the nobles and other members of the court had been transformed from the silk-adorned bureaucrats to commanders, and knights were all clad in armor or at least wearing swords and daggers, depending on their personal discipline. This pleased the old one, for now Avalon truly was of one mind and heart. They proceeded to the great hall, and there were even more attendees that had gathered from all about the Mystic realm, as the word had been sent out that the accursed had launched his assault upon all those that opposed his rule and that no one kingdom or race would be spared the horror of his lust for conquest. All turned when Lord Pirah and the high guardian Etilgam Inim entered the great hall of Avalon. Some approached while others took up positions along the walls or found seating, for the subject at hand was about to be brought to discussion.

Several members of the diocese were those that approached great Pirah and Lord Etilgam and bid him welcome. Lord Brieghlon, first council of Lady Rhona, was first to speak.

"You have no idea how glad we are to see your safe return, my lord Pirah. All will be looking to your wisdom for what is to come."

Pirah replied, addressing the group, "I'm sure all have wisdom that we shall need to rely on, my lords. Now if you will excuse me, I must speak with the lady of the lake, for there is much to do." Pirah strode away, leaving Etilgam to deal with the group of men, his eyes looking about for Lady Rhona or perhaps Quainor to bring him up to the present as to the events that occurred since he left for Argain to render aide to Aralainious in her desperate time of need. As he progressed through the crowd, he found that he was so preoccupied with seeking his companions, he scarcely noticed that three dragons had extended their long necks across the great hall, and the heads of said dragons were hovering just over him.

He looked up and smiled to see Serous Drakkus, Tarc Rocoran, and General Slovaicha. "Greetings, my friend," Serous began.

"Greetings to you as well, Serous, Tarc, and Lord General. I bring good tidings from Argain. Lady Aralainious will recover with little ill effects and be once again ready for what may come," Pirah replied.

"My lord Pirah, what know you of the past events since departing to the Dragon realm, Argain? The events that have transpired here and elsewhere?" Tarc Rocoran inquired.

Pirah looked at each of them, having a question on their faces (as Dragons could). He concluded that some things did happen that he was not aware of beyond the demise of beloved Hymmnaught. He simply posed the question: "Something happened, my friends?"

Each looked to the other until Serous spoke. "My friend, have you heard as to how Growgothal was attacked and what was done to ensure the victory over the Ogres?"

"No, good Serous, only that beloved Hymmnaught has fallen and that there has been no word from Vessiel or the court of Growgothal."

Serous paused for a moment then spoke. "As you departed for Argain to the aide of Lady Aralainious, the Centaur host, as well as a contingent of Argain, tried to portal to Growgothal but to no avail, for a powerful spell had been cast on the realm of Ogres, letting no one pass. Conjure we did, one and all, to break the spell, but nothing could lose the hold it had, and surely it could have only been the accursed as the source of its making, for even mighty Quainor and myself, your most learned students, could not break what had been cast. Lady Rhona did try to undermine the spell, but alas, it was not to be. I ordered the Argain to fly at speed to aid the Ogres and vanquish those that invade Growgothal." A crowd had formed around Pirah as well as Etilgam, nudging his way through to be at his friend's side. Quainor could be seen also moving through the crowd as well as Lady Rhona from behind the diocese; the people parted as they approached.

Serous continued. "From the keep of Avalon came forth the assassin now released from his guard sphere by your decision, my lord, and bid he make the attempt in hope of showing he would be useful and gain trust."

"You're saying Feckulis rendered aid?" Pirah asked of Drakkus.

"Indeed," said the king of Dragons.

"Tell me, my lords, how? What sort of service to those about did Lord Feckulis perform?" Drakkus once again spoke.

"Lord Feckulis, with the aid of Lord Quainor, shattered the fabric of the Mystic realm in order to break the spell that had been cast over the realm of Growgothal, my lord, by creating a monolith of enormous power and placing a great hammer in its grasp. As Lord Quainor held the portal open, the monolith struck again and again until destroying the barrier that blocked our advance. But alas, our efforts did not come in time. Lo, did we break the lines of the enemy, but the damage had been done, and as you already have heard, beloved Hymmnaught is no more."

Pirah stood thoughtful for a moment, absorbing what he was told, remembering that he had released Feckulis from his imprisonment after the attack on Avalon, giving him just enough rope to hang himself. Feckulis, on the other hand, had seen what was his position in the world and saw fit to change his allegiance to the side that would most likely give support rather than see him as disposable. It became clear that he needed to show how far he would go for his would-be allies. Pirah would go to Feckulis—once he was finished in the great gall. He looked about to see the faces of Quainor and Lady Rhona as well as the rest of the court that had gathered to hear what was transpiring with the three Dragons and the old one, and at just that moment, a waif standing next to the lady of the lake announced with a loud, shrill voice, "Will all take their rightful places in the great hall as the day's business is upon us. I give you, Lords and Generals, our beloved lady of the lake and high council of Avalon!"

The crowd began to shift and take their places at tables and various stepped levels that had been placed in the great hall at the declaration of war. The great hall of Avalon had been transformed to a place of planning and tactics, for the day-to-day lives of all involved had been changed—forever.

The discussions went on, and plans were presented with great zeal concerning invasion and the inevitable battles to come with the ideal of crushing the forces of Favlos and his allies in order to restore the peace. Pirah, all the while, thought that all this was just what he had already lived through again and again in his younger days so long ago, and always the balance was restored, but not this time; this time it was entirely different. There was no posturing of the accursed, no armies on the move toward weakened battlements used to gain tactical advantage, only raids with enormous resources piled into the fray as well as monstrous beasts and expendable constructs. Pirah decided to leave the council chamber and did so without being seen he then, left the great hall from a side entrance so as to avoid walking down the entranceway, for he had business with another.

There were guardians posted all about the palisade and the city, for obvious reasons, and so he addressed one. "Guardian, would you know where I could find Lord Feckulis?"

"Yes, my lord, he is in the infirmary at the house of healers, recovering from the deeds preformed," said the Guardian, and Pirah thanked him and proceeded to the house of healers. It took only a few moments to reach his destination and to locate Favlos in his chamber, where he lay in bed asleep, appearing exhausted and frail, as if having been very close to death yet recovering slowly. Pirah quietly approached the bed, and as he was just next to it, Favlos awoke with a start.

"*Oh!*" he exclaimed with his eyes wide open and then realized it was the old one standing next to his bed; he tried to sit up, but Pirah motioned that he not. Favlos looked at Pirah through worn and haggard eyes, his appearance reflecting the effort he had put into shattering the fabric of the Mystic realm in order to aid Growgothal and Hymmnaught.

Pirah looked back at Feckulis with curious yet sympathetic eyes and then spoke to him. "You took great risk in your task, my lord, to the point of almost ending your life. Why?"

"I found myself quite at odds my lord Pirah. The accursed has sent forces to assassinate the assassin, and although all are disposable to him when one has garnered such attention in these matters, it would be prudent to choose a side as it were. My reasoning was that if I broke the spell or at least provided some way past it, I would be proving myself useful, and if I died in the attempt, then my troubles would be over. How have I done, my lord Pirah?" Feckulis answered.

"The attempt you made indeed created a path, however, moments too late, I'm afraid. Yet the effort has not gone unnoticed. We shall speak again, my lord. Rest well for we have many more uses for you." Pirah turned and headed for the entrance to the chamber.

"Thank you, Lord Pirah. I shall endeavor to serve." Feckulis lay back in his bed, wondering just how long before assassins would come to call for him. Perhaps this very day? He thought for only a minute longer before once again exhaustion took over, and his eyes closed, pulling him into a deep sleep. Pirah left the house of healers and returned to the great hall, where he found that not much had changed in the way of progress, with some sort of plan for gathering armies that were to rout the enemy. He drew in a deep breath and let out a heavy sigh.

He motioned to Drakkus and the other two Dragons and they brought their heads over to him (wonderful thing to have such a long neck). "My friends, I believe we will be forced into taking the lead with this campaign, at least to put the lady of the lake as the voice to be heard."

"I agree," Serous Drakkus commented. Slovaicha seemed to be preoccupied, looking about having not dealt with so many different species due to the isolation of Eschrokahn Veh for so many centuries. Although he had learned much about it, he had little actual firsthand experience. Tarc Rocoran noticed.

"Somewhat different from what is the norm for Eschrokahn Veh, brother?"

"Quite, my lord, for although, in the palace of my king, there will be emissaries and some from the other realms in service, there are none so many as this," Slovaicha pointed out. The leaders of the armies of the Mystic realm, the high lords of Avalon, as well as the council continued to deliberate, some with raised voices, professing that having been involved in the last war with the accursed gave them the most experience, and therefore, they should be placed in command of the joint forces. But they were rebuffed by the other leaders, pointing out the youth and tenacity that the elders seemed to lack. Pirah caught the attention of Etilgam and motioned for him to join them.

"I believe we should call these fine people to order, my lord?" Pirah remarked in a question that was a statement.

Etilgam nodded and bellowed. "All will come to attention! Cease all bickering and come to order, for the lady of the lake shall conduct this war counsel! I say again, *come to order*!"

This had the desired effect, as all came to silence, with only a few lingering whispers and grumblings. Everyone took up positions throughout the hall, some even walking up the tails and legs of the Dragons, as there was not as much room available with so many emissaries present. Lady Rhona, Lord Quainor, and the other council members made their way to the diocese of the great hall of Avalon, the people of the court making room for them to pass. After they took their places the waif of the great hall called out in clear voice, "All hail our beloved Lady Rhona, high priestess of Avalon, duly made protector of the Mystic realm, and lady of the lake!" All in attendance placed their hands or claws over their chests and bowed. Lady Rhona stood up from her chair and did so in return.

"I will not wish good morrow this day, my lords, for there is no good to come from what we have to do and the plans we shall make this and every day forth, as life as we know has changed forever. The peace that has been for these centuries past has been breached, and by the methods being employed by the accursed, it has been made apparent the mayhem that we have witnessed as of late is only the beginning of what is to come. Old ideals may fall short of what we truly need to consider in our plans to combat this perpetual chaos being launched by what seems to be the whim of our enemy. Although there are many here that believe they should take command of this campaign, I must wait on this decision, for there are too many variables that have been produced, including the crossing over to the Mortal realm that dwells upon the face of Earth Mother. Hear me, my lords. We must not become imprisoned by our own stubbornness and lack of vision. We must meet this strategy with like strategy for there will be no epic battles, I believe."

"Then what do you propose we do in the meantime, my lady? Our forces gather. All are ready to mount attacks. Where do we find the method of these strategies you speak of?" the lord of the high mountain Shape-Shifters chimed in (able to assume the shape of canines or bears and other human-type life-forms).

"We have not as yet formed our own strategies, my lord Pathurous, so we are asking for patience, if not constructive ideas, in this dark hour."

Lord Quainor interjected. "Please excuse my outburst, my lady." Lady Rhona curtly nodded toward the overzealous Lord Quainor but dared not look directly at him for fear of exposing her feelings. At that moment, a messenger from the diocese of Fairies flew through the great doorway of the great hall and lit before the council. He was quite young as Fairies went, but one never knew with Fairies as they barely aged. He produced a tube with the markings of the high king of Fairies as well as one of the council, that being Dia-Limorain, mother to Etilgam Inim and queen water Fairy of the diocese of Fairies.

He then bowed graciously and held out the tube for Lady Rhona. The waif of the great hall took the tube and opened it, removed the parchment, and placed it in the outstretched hand of Lady Rhona. She looked to the messenger, smiling and slightly bowing, and he did the same then turned and flew from the great hall. The lady of the lake opened the scrolled parchment and read the contents then motioned for Pirah to come and read it as well. He also read the contents of the scroll, looked up at the roomful of leaders and generals of armies, and announced, "The armies of Growgothal are on the march. They do not come this way to join us. They march on Celoth, in full strength plus mercenary contingents, bringing their numbers to nearly one million. They go to annihilate the half Giants and their lord, Orokoth. It is suspected that Vessiel has laid claim to vengeance before coming to our gathered forces. The Ogres have been set to task."

There was a silence in the room for only a brief moment before the occupants began to discuss what had just been said. The voices could be heard becoming louder as those that disagreed with the choice that was made by Vessiel, queen of Ogres, suggested that treason or even grief-stricken insanity had taken over her rational thinking. It could bring her to continue to seek vengeance where there was no fault. The discussion became a roar, mingled with character insults and the possibility of less mental capacity by means of childhood head injuries. This continued until Slovaicha could stand no more bickering and let out a heart-stopping roar that brought the room to silence. "Well done," Serous Drakkus said.

"It seemed necessary at this point," Slovaicha answered. All looked to Pirah for what was to be done. What was Avalon to do about the Ogres and their solitary actions?

Rhona stood up and came close to Pirah. "What does this mean, my lord? Have the Ogres betrayed the trust we have, or is this something else?"

Pirah stood in thought for a moment and then looked to the faces of those in the great hall. "I have no answer for you, my lords and ladies, and I cannot surmise anything as of yet, but know this: I shall send emissaries to Her Majesty Queen Vessiel to ask what her true intentions are. In the meantime, I suggest we quit bickering and start planning in such a way that you have never thought of, because that is exactly what the accursed is doing as we speak."

CHAPTER 4

Alitius

He stood watching over the embankment that looked down over the road and waited for the next automobile to pass before he would step off and make his way across. As he heard the motor of an oncoming vehicle approach, a mischievous grin came across his face, and he thought, "Oh, why not? We'll be a common sight soon enough." Just as the car passed by, he stepped down the embankment within the peripheral vision of the driver and the occupant, causing them to snap their heads simultaneously in his direction. The driver slammed on the breaks, causing the tires to screech in agony as they slid down the road until coming to a stop. The driver and passenger were both in shock, staring at what no one would believe was standing in the road—an eleven-foot-tall Sasquatch that apparently waved and darted off into the surrounding forest.

The Terran biped (Sasquatch) made his way through the forest, making no noise, not even the snapping of twigs or rustle of leaves. Every so often, he looked about to see any mortals or other beings that might be trailing him as he traveled through the forest. He made sure he was not being followed by moving in broad circles always, crossing his own path, checking for footprints that were mingled with his. Continuing, he came to the place where he was to meet with his kind and stood for a moment before an open glen. The sun was going down at this time, and the trees were giving shadow to the area, creating an early darkness; he stepped out into full view and then heard a voice. "Couldn't help yourself, I suppose?" said the voice from what seemed to be from the trees.

"The temptation got the best of me, my lord, and their faces were priceless." Alitius stepped out from the tree he had blended with, a slight grin on his face, and greeted his general with an embrace.

"The wave I thought quite humorous. I don't think anyone has done that."

"Not in my lifetime," came another voice from the trees, followed by yet another and yet several other Sasquatch appearing from brush, trees, and boulders that surrounded the glen. Each of them well over ten and eleven feet tall, some even taller—great, hairy behemoths with slight variations in color and style of presentation. These were the lords of the North American bipeds that had gathered to bring what news they had of the activities they witnessed of the agents of the accursed Favlos.

As they formed a circle, the smallest of them mentioned, "Where is our lady of the south coastal lands? Will she not attend?"

Then came a voice from the very ground at the center of the circle. "I beg your pardon, my lord, but I believe the rest of you were late for this gathering. I've been here for nearly seven turns of the sun." They all looked down as the ground shifted, and up raised another great Sasquatch, only this time a female, with the stature of some of the larger beings as well as full rounded breasts and yet definite feminine features about her face.

"You've underestimated my sister, my lord—again," replied one of the group as they all chuckled. Melqua and Pawqua, who were brother and sister and ruled the western regions of what the mortals called the USA, Northern Mexico, and Canada, as well as being related to Alitius, stood next to each other. The family resemblance was unmistakable.

General Aisus, the last to arrive pointed, out the urgency of the meeting at hand and the news he did bring. The others also had tidings of what goings-on had occurred as of the last year since the finding of Pirah and the attacks within the Mystic realm. Alitius had been sent by the old one to gather what could be so as to surmise what the accursed was planning and where. The broods of the bipeds all about Earth Mother were sent word of the coming chaos that was inevitable and to provide what intelligence they could, bringing this information to Alitius, who in turn would share it with Pirah and Avalon along with her allies. Indeed, the agents of Favlos were quite industrious in their tasks, for the lords of the bipeds had much to report. The fate of those that dwelled on the face Earth Mother was indeed grim.

As it would be, the gathering went on for several days and nights, with each one of the lords and lady telling of what they had seen, and others brought messages from other parts of the world, telling of ancient terrors being resurrected from long ago that had passed into myth. Many Mortals had been recruited and had been given wealth and other physical resources to carry out the deeds they were so commanded to. On and on the testimonies came in, telling of the obvious and truly devious intentions of the enemy. Alitius took it all in and sat pondering what could be done in the meantime as they waited for word from the Mystic realm and Lord Pirah as to what plans had been made.

It became very plain to Alitius that no linear way of thinking would do in this coming fray, for there was nothing linear about what he was hearing; Pirah must come soon and be shown what was transpiring on Earth Mother and the Mortal realm and very soon, soon indeed. Alitius decided he would need to go to the far east and see for himself; he would need to travel over the polar ice caps and journey down through the frozen wastes of the northern regions that the Mortals called Russia, into Mongolia, where those that were called Yeti dwelled and at this time gathered and made plans. Then even farther south to China, to the Yeren broods and beyond, where the biped were still worshipped as Gods of the forests.

Truly the dark and dismal days to come were nearly upon them in the Mortal realm, and there was little that could be done. Alitius could feel in his very essence that this abomination being brought to them was not to be quelled—not ever. His journey would take months, and he would have to be stealthy or be discovered and have to engage mortals, which could be disastrous. Alitius thought for a moment, then all in the group of Sasquatches became silent, for an ominous rippling of the very air in the middle of the circle had manifested before them.

All knew what this meant, only not knowing who may be coming forth from the portal that was forming. Alitius, however, recognized its source immediately and stood in front of the now formed opening. The first to emerge was Quainor of the diocese of Avalon; the next to come forward was Pirah, the first, the old one. All present dropped to one knee and bowed—except Alitius. Pirah simply wouldn't have it. "Rise, my lords and my lady," the great Pirah spoke as he was embraced by Alitius. "It seems as though an age has passed since you led me to the Lock, my brother."

"More," Alitius replied.

"My coming is without plan, my friends. Our enemy has no rhyme nor reason, and so shall we. Let us hear what there is, and so we shall go forth and take in what has happened since the plans of the accursed took shape."

"My lord Pirah, this pretty one you bring, we know him not." All looked to Quainor and then Pirah, for it was true. None had seen him, for his time on Earth Mother was before the time of the Terrans.

"Truly, my lord general, you have all not met my companion. Please allow me. My lords and lady, I give you Lord Quainor, sorcerer of the highest order, master of growing matter as well as other disciplines, council member of the diocese of sacred Avalon, and one of my finest students in the Mystic arts."

General Aisus touched his pawlike hand to his chest and gave a slight bow. "My lord," said the general, as did the others, having been quite impressed by the introduction, for not likely were the praises of Lord Pirah.

Quainor returned the greeting with a slow and noble bow, and all were impressed by his demeanor; no high-born snob was this one. The gatherers let no time pass as they took up the task of what had to be done. Now that Pirah and Quainor had arrived, the time would be shortened from months to days, if not hours. Alitius explained his plan to see for himself what had been told over the last several days of the gathering and his desire to connect with the other broods of bipeds about Earth Mother, and Pirah agreed. He and Quainor then gave the other Terran lords and lady their fond adieu, and Alitius had General Aisus accompany him. With a deliberate motion of his right hand, Quainor created a portal, and the four of them vanished through it. The remaining bipeds looked about at one another and said nothing until Melqua made comment. "If the pretty one had just a little more fur about him, I think I would allow him to mount me." All laughed out loud, knowing who would be actually doing the mounting.

Then one other remarked, "I would be curious of the result of such a coupling." Then more laughter erupted with yet an answer from Melqua.

"Oh, let us not destroy a perfect moment with conception. I only am interested in the effort!" This caused an even louder eruption of laughter and then embraces as they all drifted back into the forest, for there was much still to be done, more broods to gather, to be placed and not revealed.

On the other side of the world, high in the Himalayan mountains, the portal opened with the familiar shimmering of the air, followed by an opening that, for all reasons, came out of nowhere. Alitius stepped out first, followed by Pirah, then Quainor and Aisus. The air was very cold, near freezing, as it wasn't quite winter yet, and the sky had some clouds but was mostly blue while the sun was at midmorning. The portal closed when commanded by Quainor, and all looked about for signs of humans or other beings that might be lurking about, as just as they were scouting the world on the surface of Earth Mother, so would be the enemy. Alitius drew a deep breath and exhaled, and as he did, so did Aisus; they both looked at each other with a slight shake of their heads, and Alitius spoke.

"There are none here." He then drew in yet another deep breath and let out a bellowing yell that sounded like a loud moan coupled with a roar. The mountains echoed this call for some time, reverberating again and again until finally going silent. The four of them stood silently, waiting for some sort response, yet there was none—at least not right away. Quainor had a very puzzled look on his face, trying to see or hear anything that might be a sign of the Terrans that they were seeking out, and then it came to him that there just may not be any to seek out at all.

"My lord, I have a suspicion that something is very wrong and that we should press on and investigate," said Quainor.

"For some, my lord, this would seem apparent, but these times would garner prudence for those we seek. Let us practice patience," Alitius replied. Another five minutes passed and still nothing from the Yeti who dwelled in these lands. Aisus also began to suspect that something was amiss and reiterated Quainor's suggestion to investigate. Pirah, who had remained silent for the most part, simply met Alitius's gaze and nodded in agreement.

"Very well, let us seek out our brethren and discover what is and what is not," said Alitius.

The four of them set out. As they walked, the two sorcerers made slight gestures, and their clothing became augmented with warm coats and the attire of modern-day humans. The Sasquatch moved in the trees and kept vigilant for signs of Yeti or any other beings that may be roaming about, ever ready to blend in with the surroundings without notice. Their search seemed to be almost in vain as there was nothing to indicate any activity of broods or otherwise, yet the four pressed on, for it was just that lack of activity that only a Terran would see as raising suspicion to higher levels, and the need to find the truth about this grew. Onward they looked, and still no indication of Yeti or past meetings of them. Then General Aisus made a very strong point.

"They do not want to be found, my lords." Silently they all looked to one another; their expressions were enough confirmation that indeed it was the case—the Yeti were hiding from something that was enough to provoke them to not be found even by friends.

"Then how shall we contact them?" Quainor asked.

"I am certain they will contact us, my lord Quainor, for our presence has not gone unnoticed by the forests and those that call them home. It will simply be a bit longer, but not much, I think," Alitius replied. A great smile came over the Sasquatch lord's face as he looked past Pirah and Quainor to a far peak, where at first there was nothing, then a lone figure stood from a boulder, a shaggy large white figure.

Aisus also caught sight of the figure so far away yet well within the sight and hearing abilities of the Terrans and their cousin broods. The Yeti stood for a moment and then disappeared behind the same boulder, but only for a moment. Now all four were focusing on the peak where the figure had been noticed, and just then, two more appeared, both looking directly at them. One could be seen lifting his arm to his face and leaning back, then but a few seconds passed, and a long moaning roar filled the air around them. The call of the Yeti—for centuries it froze the hearts of indigenous people of the Himalayas and those from foreign lands that would try to explore this ancient and unyielding country. Alitius inhaled, and just before he could let out his response, a voice came from what seemed like thin air—a voice with a distinct ancient, a Tibetan speech nuance.

"You needn't shout, my lord. We are here." No sooner did the voice speak than at least twenty of the Yeti that made up the "we" statement appeared from trees and the snow-covered banks that made up the landscape that they all stood upon, and as each became visible, they bowed to Alitius and Aisus then to Pirah and Quainor.

"How did you conceal yourselves so completely that we could not detect your presence, brothers?" inquired Aisus as he moved to embrace the first who had spoken. The first Yeti with a solemn look on his face explained. "It was necessary to employ our oldest techniques of slowing the blood flow and allowing the cold to alter our external layers of fur, skin, and fat so as to emit no scent or change the temperature of the stones and plants we become one with. For the enemy had found ways to detect us otherwise."

"This has not happened in the west as of yet, my lord. Have you discovered how it is done?" Aisus inquired.

"No, my lord, we've not. Only have we discovered that the enemy has been hard at work building his strength on the face of the world and is poised at this very moment to strike with the most powerful beasts and those from long ago that have been reawakened and scores of savage brutes that have been concealed—all of this made possible by mortals that have been recruited by agents of the accursed from the mystic realm. They are many, my lord, as many as the leaves that cover the forests in spring."

"Forgive me, brother, but we have never met. I am Alitius of the northern broods of the American continent, and these are my companions, General Aisus, also of the same and—"

The Yeti interrupted. "Lord Pirah of the Mystic realm, creator of many, the first, the old one, keeper of balance, and mentor to us all. Your names and legacy are as a herald, my lord." Pirah placed his right fist into is left palm and bowed at the hip. "But who is this one? So quiet yet paying so much attention."

Quainor also placed his right fist to his left palm and introduced himself. "I am Quainor, high counsel to the diocese of Avalon, mystic of growing things, and companion to the old one—and at your service, my friends."

"Please, if you will allow me," a second Yeti spoke and motioned with his hand. "This, my brothers, is Lord Sin Feng, highest of our brood. I am Lord Kang Lo, second to Sin Feng. These two are our honored commanders, General Fong Lu Xeng and Capitan Shin. I'm afraid the rest would take quite an age to introduce, but rest assured, they are of the same heart." Kang Lo bowed and stood back.

"We are truly honored, brothers, for being in your presence at this time, but I am afraid we must get to the business at hand. What have you discovered about the activities of the agents of the accursed, and what sort of conjuring have you witnessed?" Pirah asked. Sin Feng gestured that they all sit while Capitan Shin gave silent orders through hand signals to the remaining Yeti, who stepped into the surroundings and disappeared.

Sin Feng began. "What we have seen and experienced in regard to the activities of those in league with the accursed is most disturbing, my lord Pirah, most disturbing, for the numbers are quite staggering from both the Mystic realm and the ranks of human mortals of this fifth age who have been seduced by the gain of power and riches. He has been able to recruit those that are of angry hearts and greedy minds that have been impressed by the powers displayed by the Mystics of his very court at Corsolvess. These are but what we have discovered in these regions. We've heard nothing from other parts of Earth Mother." Pirah sat silently for a moment, considering what he had just heard, then asked Alitius.

"There have been no such sightings in the Americas, brother?"

"This would be the reason I needed to come to this place, my lord, for the broods of the Americas made similar reports, although no contact with the growing numbers as mentioned, nor have we been discovered by any of those that may see us when we meld with the flora and fauna of our surroundings. I believe it is only a matter of time."

Pirah only took a few seconds before he spoke. "My lord, you must go back to the Americas and warn all of the broods, for I fear the time is now, and they must find ways to remain concealed until we can bring forth our own numbers, and for this I am going to go forth and revisit the Gods of old to see if I might convince them to bring their legions into the fray. This I am not certain of as they have been unconcerned with the affairs of men since the time of the Nazarene and the Roman insurrection."

"If I may, my lord Pirah, the worshipers of the Hindu Gods still hold true to the ancient ways as well as some factions in Cathay [China] and Nippon," said General Xeng.

"Are there not those here in Tibet that still see the Yeti as Gods?" inquired Alitius. The Yeti all grinned, seeing the humor in the question, and just as Sin Feng was about to speak, there was the cracking and rattling of semi- and fully automatic gunfire from not too far off. All were fully alert as there was also the crashing of trees and the sound of bullets striking metal just inside the tree line. The sound of personal combat was heard with the clashing of weapons and the all-too-familiar snarl of what could only be one creature—a Troll. The melee came to an abrupt halt; seconds passed before a huge Yeti appeared, his white fur blotched with the gray-green blood of the Troll he had just slain. In his right hand was a great Pao Dao, and in his left hand was the head of his adversary, which he held for all to see.

"This piece of ox dung and more like him are mixed with the troops of Cathay. My lords, they are upon us. You must go." Aisus reacted first by breaking a long, stout branch from a tree and tearing the twigs from it in one motion. Aisus would be armed and would fight to the last if need be.

Just as he braced himself for the impending onslaught, Pirah opened a portal and exclaimed, "You must get back to your broods and make haste. This could start anew in your lands. *Go!*" The area where they stood suddenly erupted with Trolls and Mortals with automatic rifles and RPG launchers. At the same moment, an untold number of Yetis emerged from the trees and rocks. The battle was on with vicious tenacity from both contingents. The Yeti swung their Pao Dao and oversized broadswords, cutting the Mortals down before they could bring their weapons to bear as well as engaging the Trolls, who were similarly armed with axes, spears, and swords.

Those that charged the high lords were met with wide, deep pits opening under them and just as quickly buried alive by the power of Lord Quainor of Avalon. Sin Feng produced two short machetes (Chinese short broadsword) and cut the heads off two Trolls that saw him as old and defenseless. He looked to Pirah as Alitius and Aisus vanished through the portal and spoke as calmly as the first time they met. "Go, my lord Pirah. We shall make our egress in good time. You must escape to the Mystic realm and prepare your return, and you may want to bring many more with you—many." Pirah nodded. At just that moment, the brush erupted with more enemies. Pirah's eyes became bright yellow, and he pointed his open palm at the new threat. A ball of plasma fire shot from his hand, and the mass of Troll and Mortal was obliterated, leaving body parts and entrails scattered about.

Hoping he bought them time, he could hear the automatic rifle fire as he stepped through the portal. Pirah would make those in league with Favlos pay dearly for what was happening in Tibet. In the earlier times of his stewardship to Earth Mother, he had become quite fond of those regions and the ways of its inhabitants. Sin Feng had reminded him of those times and the beauty that was old Cathay.

CHAPTER 5

The Oath of Feckulis, the Mikro Vadakos, Pirah Means to Strike

Upon returning to Avalon, Pirah and Quainor lost no time, calling a council meeting to prepare for what was coming both in the Mystic realm and the face of Earth Mother and the Mortal world. All would be summoned; there would be none that would be spared, for the accursed had made good with his time and created untold numbers of construct and mortal conscript. The mystics that had sworn their allegiance to Favlos were already in place in the world of mortals and had created their own followings, setting themselves as Gods to the weaker minded. The battle for Earth Mother and balance may have already been lost, and so they must continue to be ready for war. The attendees of the council meeting of the great hall of Avalon had swelled to greater numbers with the arrival of the many banners and their kings, queens, and lords. The outlying areas that surrounded sacred Avalon seemed to be alive with rows and rows of tents and several temporary palisades for the previously mentioned heads of state.

All had heard the call for a meeting by great Pirah, who had returned from the Mortal realm with news of what transpired over the last fifty or more years on the face of Earth Mother. All made their way to the great hall through the streets of sacred Avalon that had begun to transform from a city of light and beauty to a fortress with fortifications and supplies if a siege were to take place with armed civilians as well as guardians, Centaurs, and Fairies; however, the Dwarves had not shown yet. Other forms were just arriving in the realm of Avalon but had not yet reached the gates of the city. When the great hall had reached its capacity, there were those still outside on the palisade, and so runners were dispatched, with scrolls of what had been discussed. At times certain lords were summoned to the great hall for their particular insights and expertise. The one thing that had become certain was that Earth Mother must be taken back, or at best a balance of what was happening must be created, or this would only be the beginning of the chaos that Favlos was so obviously going to bring to every realm.

Feckulis, having fully recovered from his exhausted state, was walking the grounds and observing the swelling of the populace, wondering where he might fit in or if his previous ignominy had been forgiven by those of Avalon. As he walked among the people, there were no jeers or scowls, just an evenness of being, and when he made eye contact with those that knew his stature, he was greeted with "My lord" and a curt bow.

He reflected on the past months and how he had come to where he was in this unfolding and perpetual drama that for all purposes has destroyed the way of life in the Mystic realm and continued in the Realm of mortals on the face of Earth Mother. He glances about suddenly and noticed that there was no sphere shadowing his every movement. Apparently, Lord Pirah was giving him the chance to be a part of the efforts of Avalon and kind or hang himself by being treacherous. He was just thinking of what he could do in these trying times that would shore up his standing when he caught eye of Lady Bah Di Ah Aziza headed to the archery range with bow in hand and a quiver of arrows across her back. He was struck by her beauty and height, as most were when first seeing her. She was looking about for something unknown when she caught Feckulis looking at her. Though he, at first, was going to look away, he didn't. She looked at him with a curious tilt of the head and then a brief smile. He gave her a curt nod and touched his hand to his chest, then proceeded through the crowd. Feckulis found him at odds, for he detected something strange about the statuesque lady elf that seemed as though she had walked from a dream. There was something very familiar that he couldn't quite identify.

He would address this the next time he saw her, but for now, Feckulis needed to find Lord Pirah. He decided that the palisade would be a good place to start and headed in that direction, making his way through the crowd that seemed to grow in density as he came closer to his intended destination, and so his progress became ever slower. He thought very seriously of simply dematerializing and reconstituting near the palisade, but then he thought, "No, this would only be construed as an attack by the accursed." Then he would find himself being obliterated or worse by the forces of Avalon. He decided to simply move with the crowd, and just then, he felt a presence looming over him from behind.

"Good day, my lord Feckulis," said a voice that was soft yet deep and alluring. He whirled around to find himself inches away from the breastplate of the very tall, beautiful, and pleasant-smelling Lady Badi Ah Aziza. He had to lean his head back to look up at her face and was struck once again by her almost inconceivable magnificence.

"Good day to you as well, my lady. I'm afraid you have me at a disadvantage. We've not been introduced. Please, if you would, I am Feckulis, Mystic and assassin—although these days I'm not sure if the latter is true or not. However, that is what I've been. Yet at this moment, I am your humble servant."

The statuesque elf did a half curtsy with a tilt of her head and said, "I am Badi Ah Aziza, ward to the old one, student to Lord Inim, and lady to the court of Avalon and Argain. My lord Feckulis." He stood transfixed, looking into her eyes that seemed to hypnotize him with their kaleidoscopic appearance and the fairness of her skin. He found himself overtaken by her. She spoke to him and broke the spell. "I couldn't help but notice you just a moment ago, and I was struck curious as to what you were doing this fine day."

Feckulis composed himself and replied, "Truly, my lady, I was captured by your visage, but a moment earlier, I was off to the palisade to speak with Lord Pirah to see what I can do to further my uses in this cause."

"I see. Perhaps I can be of some assistance in your progress, my lord." Badi Ah raised her hand, and the crowd parted, allowing Feckulis to walk directly to the palisade without encumbrance. He looked up at her, realizing that the congestion was indeed her doing so as to make this meeting with him, but for what purpose?

"I am pleased to have made your acquaintance, my lady," he said then proceeded to the palisade. Bah Di Ah watched him with a curious stare until he was far away yet still in view. A slight smile formed on her sensual full lips, and she wheeled around to continue to the archery range. Feckulis also continued onto the palisade to find Lord Pirah and affirm his choice to be a part of the conflict in the service of those that opposed his former master. However, he could not seem to put the encounter with Lady Bah Di Ah out of mind—not for a second.

When he came to the steps of the palisade, there were hundreds, if not thousands, of people of many species about, all looking like warriors or of some high station, some conversing most, moving about from place to place. He didn't know exactly what he was going to say once he found Pirah, only that he had found himself in a most peculiar state of being and that his ways of the assassin were no longer viable—not in the service of the enemy at least. As he climbed the steps to the broad area before the great hall, he noticed a young girl standing at the entrance who seemed to have some authority, and so he walked toward her in hopes she may provide him with some direction. As he approached, the keepers of the great hall took a guarded stance, both with their axes ready to dash the mystic into pulp if he took another step. The waif regarded Feckulis with more than a hint of disapproval. He looked up at the keepers then at the waif and, for a moment, felt like he could conjure his own giant stone creatures, and they could have at it, but good sense told him it was not a good course of action, and so he chose another path. As the waif took a step toward him, he dropped to one knee and, in his best ingratiating voice, spoke. "My dear lady, I beseech you, stay the keepers but for a moment, for I mean no harm or encroachment. I only wish to ask but a single question of need." He then bowed his head, waiting for the young waif to reply.

"Careful, sorcerer, I know who you are, and though you may have fallen under the good graces of the old one, you have much to prove to me. The attack that was meant to claim you claimed my beloved teacher Mahran, and I have not found forgiveness as of yet."

Feckulis remained on one knee, and with his face looking down, he said, "I am truly sorry for your loss, my lady, as well as for those that were lost during the raid by the forces that were in league with my former master, which brings me to the question that I came to ask."

The waif stood looking very imperiously at the former prisoner, now guest of Avalon, considering what her next answer would be for this humble yet questionable man. "Very well, sorcerer, ask your question."

"I am searching for the old one himself to inquire what service I may provide and further secure my place among those that unite against the accursed self-proclaimed God king of the realm of Mystics and those realms under the stewardship of great Pirah."

The waif stood, once again looking quite imperious but only to continue her moment of superiority, and just as Feckulis was about to continue, she interjected. "Lord Pirah walks the battlements with Lord Etilgam, Lord Quainor, and Lord Pathurous."

"Thank you, my gracious lady." Feckulis waited for the name of his benefactor and looked at her with a patient smile.

"Gloria, my name is Gloria, my lord, waif to the council hall."

"My lady Gloria," said Feckulis. He then whirled about and made his way once again through the crowd toward the closest access to the outer walls of sacred Avalon.

Gloria stood watching him walk away and looked at the keepers that were already at ease. "He's not really such a bad sort, is he?" The keepers simply looked at her with no expression then looked on. "Oh, never mind."

Pirah and company were observing the fortifications inside and out of the city walls, taking notice of the array of trenches lined with pikes and obstacles that would thwart a movement of Trolls and other large beings if that would be the engagement. Contingents of Dragons from Eschrokahn Veh and Argain arrived earlier, and the skies were dotted with flights of messengers and patrols overlapping one another from points far from the walls of Avalon. Feckulis spotted the four Lords and made his way over to where they stood, trying not to bump anyone as he hurriedly walked. Pirah noticed Feckulis and greeted him with some surprise. "My lord Feckulis! What brings you to these high walls at this time?"

"My lord Pirah and most honorable company, I come to you to express my most sincere sorrow for what happened as the result of the raid that was to claim my life and failed yet caused the loss of so many and the damage to this beautiful city, and also to ask of you and the many that have flocked to the banners of Sacred Avalon what service I may provide in your endeavors. Let there be no limit to what end that service takes me." The four looked at one another then to Feckulis. Etilgam Inim spoke first. "Are we hearing you correctly, lord assassin? You are pledging your powers and abilities to the struggle against your former master, the accursed Favlos and his allies?"

"I am, high guardian of Avalon," he answered.

"To whatever end that may take you?" asked Pathurous.

"To my own end, if that is where it takes me, my lords," answered Feckulis.

"You swear this before us now from this day to your last day, my lord Feckulis?" asked Pirah. Feckulis lowered himself to one knee, and as he did, he wondered how this came to be, for he was not searching out the old one to swear his fealty and never-ending allegiance but only to see what he could do to aid in their cause. Something compelled him, something he had not reckoned that would surface from within him.

"I, Feckulis, sorcerer and Mystic and assassin, forsake all that I have been and embrace only that which I shall be. I pledge my being to Lord Pirah and those he calls friend and ally and will bring to the forefront all of my abilities, be they magical or otherwise, from this day to my last day. This do I swear by the Greater Powers that create us all."

Pirah stepped forward and bid that Feckulis rise and be recognized, for the attention of his action had been great along the battlement. "I accept, Mystic, but know this. You will be held to the highest scrutiny amongst us, and any treachery will be treated with the utmost severity," said Pirah.

Feckulis stood quietly for a moment then asked, "This doesn't mean I can't have a go with a woman every now and again, does it?"

Pirah chuckled then answered, "Come now, my lord. We are not Mortals that lie to ourselves about chastity and so forth." The five of them laughed, as well as the crowd that formed to see what was thought to never be seen—the assassin Feckulis being brought into the fold by none other than the first.

At that moment, there was a commotion in the outlying palisades and rows of tents that made up all the armies that had gathered, yet it was not a call to arms but a spectacle that was approaching sacred Avalon from the west. The sound of drums and horns in rhythmic cadence slowly became louder and louder, along with sounds of marching heavily laden boots of short yet thickly muscled beings, fully armed and adorned for battle with sword, dagger, hatchet, ax, and shield. Every other warrior sported a pike at least two and one-half meters in length. At the very forefront of the seemingly endless formation was none other than Percival Ownbraw, son of Lambute Ownbraw, high lord and king over Meraan Mountain.

Pirah looked to Etilgam and spoke. "My lord high guardian, behold, your kinsmen come."

"Aye, better late than never." Etilgam snorted. Feckulis stood alongside the others, watching the columns of Dwarfs approach the city and the many other armies showing welcome by lining the road and cheering. He felt that even though he had been brought into the fray on the side of those that opposed his former master, he should bring more to the table as it were. He excused himself, explaining he had work to do, and made his egress.

Pathurous spoke. "Forgive me, my lords, but I have little knowledge of that one. Who is he exactly?"

"He is, or more accurately, was an assassin once strictly for hire for the first two ages of man on the face of Earth Mother and farther back in the realm of Mystics that we call home—until he was taken and made servant to the forebears of the accursed Favlos, and so was he to Favlos until late," said Pirah.

"His name, does it not describe decay and foul matter?" inquired Pathurous.

"Yes, his name, that would be something to muse over," Pirah answered, as well as thinking out loud. The group continued their walk about the battlements, observing the movements of the Eschrokahn Veh along with the Argain.

As they were about to conclude their discussion on defenses and move on to more aggressive tactics, a group of Guardians approached with what looked like a small Dragon among them being escorted through the crowd. The leader of the group signaled for them to halt and motioned to the Dragon to come with him. The beast stood nearly eight feet from the ground to its head, with another eight feet of tail behind him; his wings were tucked along his spine but protruded enough to add to his girth. His coloring was quite unique, more of earth tones and blended forest hues, and his eyes were quite reptilian, unlike the single-colored eyes of the larger breeds about sacred Avalon.

The guardian in charge presented the Dragon to the group of Nobles gathered at the wall. "My Lords, I give you Lord Ige'tis of the Mikro Vadakos from the southeastern forest realms." The Dragon bowed graciously, as did the others in return.

Pirah spoke. "Greetings, my lord Ige'tis. I am ever so glad to see you here. What may we of Avalon do for you?"

"It is not what Avalon can do for myself. It is what we, the Mikro Vadakos, can do for those of Avalon."

Pirah smiled and Etilgam spoke. "Welcome to the fray, brother!" The lords of Avalon, as well as the visiting lords, exchanged introductions and continued their discussions on the defensive measures taken to maintain the security of Avalon and the surrounding realms.

Ige'tis kept quiet for the most part but then found himself thinking out loud. "What of attack?"

The other lords stopped abruptly and looked to Ige'tis. "We had concentrated solely on shoring up defenses that we neglected any other options, my lord," said Quainor. The other Lords all agreed, and great Pirah couldn't hold back his grin, as though seeing the closed focus in himself.

"Behold the clarity of new eyes!" exclaimed Etilgam Inim as he placed his hand over his breastplate and bowed to Ige'tis.

Pirah spoke. "Yes, let us discuss a different tactic to meet the different tactic of our adversary."

Pathurous interjected. "I am inclined to attack with great numbers both from the air and ground, with attention to the forces that roam the seas in Favlos's service."

Quainor responded, "You speak of the navies of the accursed?"

"Yes, my lord, I do. There are other forces that have made a pact with him as well. The pirate queen Algala, sorceress and harlot, that continues to stretch the bounds of treachery with no end."

"Algala? She's been out of reach for some time, not since the last incursion," said Etilgam.

Pirah spoke, only this time with authority. "We shall attack, my lords, with near full strength, but who shall receive our brutal visit? Corsolvess? The realm of Celoth? Perhaps the Borians or the she pirate and her fleet? We must strike decisively, my friends, or Favlos has once more won the day." All stood in silence, contemplating what had been discussed and what would be the most devastating to Favlos.

"Let us not forget that Queen Vessiel is set about the destruction of the Celoth and their high lord. In itself, it will be a massive blow to the enemy," Quainor exclaimed.

"Only if the attempt is successful. Otherwise, it will be a battle to be dealt with," replied Etilgam. Pirah thought for a moment then raised his hand to the air with a flash, summoning a messenger of the Argain to come down from his formation. With a slight dip of his wings then closing them to his body, the Dragon dove with great speed to the position on the wall where the group stood. Then with incredible precision, he opened his wings, pulling up just at the wall without as much as a leaf stirring on the ground.

"Captain, I need to know what Queen Vessiel is intending with her armies on the march. The host of Growgothal is nearly or has already crossed the borders of Celoth by now. Go to her. Ask her if she intends on rejoining our efforts. Or does she have other plans? If she does not give a definitive reply, then perhaps some discreet observation may bear something for us to go on."

The captain replied, "It shall be done, my lord." Then with a single stroke of his powerful wings, he took to the air and roared a command, and two other Dragons followed him.

Pirah watched as the Argain messengers slowly disappeared to the north. "I believe, my lords, that the hammer stroke of Favlos will be on the face of Earth Mother and that anything we encounter in the realm of Mystics will be a distraction or, at best, ongoing defensive maneuvering designed to split our forces and create more internal chaos."

While this was transpiring, Tarc Rocoran had approached on the ground just outside the wall. As he stopped where the others were standing, he arched his long neck as to bring his head to the level of the group of lords on the wall. "Tell me, Lord Tarc. What say you as the escort of Drakkus, king of Dragons, and his trusted adviser? What counsel would you provide as to attacking the accursed and his forces?" asked Pirah.

"I believe for myself, my lords, that I would be as direct and invasive as could be. Open multiple portals on the face of Earth Mother, and have our various forces pour through them and engage the detritus with great prejudice and unending carnage, for that is what they will do as well to the Mortals. But alas, it simply cannot be, for there are more levels of deception than we know, and this could bring about our downfall."

Pirah nodded in agreement then looked to Quainor. "We will hold council with the lady of the lake and begin our own incursion on the face of Earth Mother. We've wasted too much time, and I fear the enemy has the upper hand already."

"If what was witnessed in the Himalayas is any indication, I see it obvious that those soldiers of Cathay have been training with forces of the Accursed for some time as they provided support, and in no way were they hindered by the appearance of Trolls or Terrans. However, I don't think they were prepared to confront Wizards. That being said, I believe that we may have to consider Lord Rocoran's option," Quainor added.

Pirah thought for a moment, considering what had been offered, then looked to Quainor. "Perhaps the soldiers were only a small part of the armies of Cathay? In those remote areas, a commander could operate as a warlord apart from the rest of the command structure. In any case, we must increase our presents on the face of Earth Mother. I would prefer clandestinely. However, we may indeed need to take invasive and overt action. This could be the end of the fifth age of humans, and quite possibly the sixth may be an age of constant chaos and destruction."

CHAPTER 6

The Gods

"**Y**ou are certain of this, my lord Pirah?"

"I am, my lady. I believe it will be quite necessary to bring as many of the Gods to this encounter as possible, for I also believe that the enemy will do the same." Pirah and Lady Rhona stood on a balcony that looked down upon sacred Avalon, discussing what was yet to come.

"What of the limitation, my lord? Has the accursed found a royal of the old ways to serve or otherwise manipulate to his end?"

Pirah sat for a moment then answered, "Of that I am not entirely certain, yet if he had, it would be quite obvious. I, on the other hand, have sent emissaries to the region of ancient Cimmeria to locate quite possibly the last of the bloodline of Nomock, king of Greacia."

"I remember the tales of Nomock that you told me and the others when I was just a waif so long ago, good Pirah."

Pirah smiled and recalled the stories in his mind but then came to what was the task that he must set about doing. "I go now to Olympus and the circle of Gods. I must confront Zeus and Hera to hopefully sway them to our cause."

"Do you take Lord Quainor with you, my lord?" Rhona questioned.

"I do not. I think he would do better to speak to the Spirit Gods of the north and south continents that were formed from the great upheaval, the Americas, for he commands the elements of growing things that which the Spirits love."

Rhona looked thoughtful for a moment, trying not to expose her feelings, then asked, "What of the Norse Gods? The All Father? Will there be council with the Aesir?"

Pirah looked into Rhona's eyes dourly, which caused her blood to run cold, then spoke, "Yes, my lady, although I'm sure convincing Odin and the rest will be the hardest of my efforts for, it was man that walked from them by corrosion from the armies that corrupted the ways of the Nazarene, turning the followers of paganism to Christianism by means of force or purchase. I will go to Asgard myself. Perhaps this should be my first task. Yes, I believe so."

"What of Olympus, my lord?" Pirah thought for a moment and smiled.

"Zeus doth sway to beauty, does he not, my lady?"

Rhona smiled and replied, "Tall beauty, I would imagine." They both laughed, and Pirah bid the lady of the lake farewell and left the balcony.

Lady Rhona then left as well and made her way from the escarpments of her dwelling to the lower chambers. Her personal guard was standing at attention at the entrance, then as she stepped outside, they all fell into place, keeping stride with her as she proceeded to the great hall of Avalon, where the other high lords were gathering for further plans, including a massive incursion on the face of Earth Mother. Lady Rhona spied Bah Di Ah Aziza and made eye contact, then bid her to come to her. She did so with grace and stealthy stride until standing in front of the lady of the lake. She then dropped to one knee, not only in showing deference but also so she would not have to look up at Bah Di Ah.

Lady Rhona then spoke. "Lord Pirah and I have a task for you, my lady." Bah Di Ah gave a somewhat crooked smile.

Pirah left the great hall and began searching out Quainor to instruct him on his task and that he should select companions and escorts for the journey. As he searched, he came upon Gloria, the waif of the great hall of Avalon, peering around the corner of a building, trying not to be seen by someone. Pirah could not make out who it was until he stood right behind her. Some ten meters from her vantage point, in the middle of a small courtyard, was Feckulis, newly brought to the fold of Avalon and allied to Pirah. Feckulis was practicing his art of creating apparitions and vicious beings that once served him as an assassin, and as he did, he would stop and look at these things that have been his stock in trade and then dispatched them with a wave of his hand.

He found himself at a quandary about how to affect his new life without bringing in the old way. He then thought deeply of an image that he found quite pleasant, and this brought a grin to his face, and then he laughed inside, dismissing his idea as folly, telling himself, "She would never see me as such." He then began to conjure something anew when came a voice.

"Good morrow, wizard. How fair you this day?"

Feckulis stopped what he was doing to address the voice that was Great Pirah himself, simultaneously startling young Gloria, who stumbled from behind her concealment.

"Good morrow to you as well, old one. And what have we here? A curious waif of the great hall?"

"Hello, Lord Feckulis, and good morrow," said Gloria.

"So what sort of scheming were you up to whilst I was practicing my trade?" asked Feckulis of Gloria.

"I was merely observing, my lord, keeping an eye on you for the sake of Avalon."

"Indeed," said Pirah.

"I must be about my duties now. I have no time for pleasantries and doings of wizards." Gloria wheeled about and dashed off toward the great hall, looking back to see if she was being observed herself.

Pirah then addressed Feckulis. "My lord, I have something in the name of our endeavors for you to do if you feel up to it."

Feckulis stood straight and looked Pirah directly in the eye. "My Lord, you have only to speak it, and I shall gratefully accept."

"I am sending envoy to the Gods of Olympus, and I would like you to accompany them," said Pirah.

Feckulis bowed graciously then asked, "Who do I have the pleasure of taking this task with, my lord?

"I believe you know her, Lord Feckulis, Lady Bah Di Ah Aziza." Feckulis noticeably reacted to the name and was taken aback for the moment; this was also noticed by Pirah. "Steady, good wizard. She has that effect on just about everyone."

Pirah bowed then made his exit from the small courtyard and made his way to his own dwelling in sacred Avalon to make ready for his part in this task as well. He thought deeply of how he would approach the All Father, Odin, and the myriad of Gods that once reigned supreme to the north men before the Christian incursion. Hopefully, there were still those that would hold true to the old ways, and Pirah may bring that to the table and convince Asgard to join the fray. The other thoughts that filled his mind were those of the Gods of the Hindu, as well as Egypt and so many others. This was going to be a task of enormous undertaking and would give the enemy too much time to have his way on Earth Mother. He must attempt to bring them together in one place, as many as he could without the accursed finding out and infiltrating the meeting. Perhaps he would use an old friend to accomplish this. He would seek out the most beloved of druids, Merlyn.

As it happened, the old wizard chose not to live in the Mystic realm at all but as a Mortal on the face of Earth Mother, in his beloved Scotland, as the owner of a souvenir shop in Glastonbury, not what one would expect from such a prominent figure in the folklore of the British Isles, but then again, Pirah himself chose a similar life for different reasons. There was no time to delay; he had to get these plans in motion, and so he went the great hall just outside and hailed the keepers to come to him; he looked intently at his right palm, and a parchment appeared, to which he began to speak. The parchment formed the words on itself and, upon his finishing his statement, rolled and sealed itself with his sigil. He then handed the message to the keeper of the left door and said, "For the lady of the lake," then departed the palisade, striding with purpose as he created a portal and stepped through it.

This action, although common for the for the dwellers of Avalon to see, was paid particular notice by a young man, or what appeared to be a young man who was just meandering about the palisade. He looked about casually to see if anyone was paying notice to him and then turned, unhurriedly walking away from the place of gathering toward the entrance gate of sacred Avalon. He took great care to make sure that he was not noticed or followed, taking different side streets and stopping to browse at one shop or another. He then made his way ever closer to the main gate, all the while noticing that the number of guardians and other warriors seemed to grow, and thus being noticed became more and more of a reality.

Just as he was about to approach the gate, one of the Centaurs recruited to the guardians began to sniff the air as if something fowl had come close to him. He looked around the people and other beings that were coming and going, trying to find the source of the offensive odor. He turned to his companion, a Centauress, who also detected the smell and was also scanning the crowd. At once they both looked at the young man and shouted, "*Halt!* Or be taken down!" The young man froze but a second and took to running through the crowd, hoping the mass of bodies would shield him, but to no avail. The Centaurs had found their mark and would not let him get away. The crowd, at first confused, was darting to and fro, not knowing how to react, but as the Centaurs gave chase, they beckoned the crowd to make way!

This was the man's downfall as the crowd parted and huddled against the walls of the buildings lining the streets, and as he tried to get between them at alleyways, he was met with a fist from one of the good people of Avalon. As the Centaurs came ever closer, he found himself trapped and in need of an escape that his pursuers did not count on.

He looked about especially toward the ground to find a way out. He did. Just some few meters from him was storm drain, covered with an iron grill and choked with debris from the run off the streets; he took two strides and stood next to it. The guardians were nearly upon him; he looked them both in the eyes as his body became shapeless and ran down the drain.

The two Centaurs looked at each other with annoyed scowls on their faces. The male turned and galloped off to report what happened while the female scanned the crowd once more, reared up on her hind legs, and with a thunderous return, pounded the ground beneath her fore hoofs in frustration. She then followed her brother at arms in a slightly more hurried gallop.

Pirah stepped through the portal he had created and once again set foot on Earth Mother, only this time he was back in the isle of Britain—

Scotland, to be precise, on a damp and somewhat foggy street in the beautiful township of Glastonbury. There he looked about and found that every other door was a souvenir shop or historical location depicting the "days of old," as it were for those who didn't know better. Pirah chuckled as he went about looking for the one shop that had his old friend and student playing the part of just another Scottish shopkeeper making his way in this world.

As he walked, he noticed that the other folk who were strolling up and down the street were looking at him strangely until one pretty young lady walked up and asked, "Can I get a selfie?" in a decidedly American dialect. He realized he was still in the garb of a Mystic. He agreed and decided to play the part of a character in period clothing for a few moments and then continued down the street. With a gesture of his right hand, his clothing transformed to current-day men's fashion—with distinguishing style. The requests for selfies then declined, and he proceeded without any further encounters—and none too soon, for he found what he was looking for in a small storefront with the word Merlyn's Citadel hand painted on the glass door window.

Pirah thought to himself, "In plain sight." He entered the small door, only to walk into a much larger room than what one would imagine from outside the establishment, with the walls covered in hide and tapestries, shields, and various weapons from so long ago; there were tables with ever so many vials and scrolls with writing in languages that only someone who lived over several thousand years ago could possibly read and comprehend. There were maps painted on hide, depicting the surface of Earth Mother during the third, fourth, and fifth ages of humans. (The proprietor of the shop was born just before the third age.) Pirah gazed about the shop in sublime reflection of a time that he was surely missing and of those past that he was most fond.

At the other end of the shop, he noticed the shopkeeper in conversation with some customers who were ever so immersed in the accent and mannerism of the proprietor of the establishment. The exchange ended with "Thank you and dae comeback wei your next visit ta thee most beautiful land a man could place his foot on" (in heavy Scottish burr).

The customers laughed and assured the man behind the counter that this would be their first stop when they returned from Arkansas to reconnect with their Scottish roots. Pirah feigned the appearance of being engrossed in an object that had been sealed in stasis in a glass jar that looked like the skull of an infant Dragon, of all things. The shopkeeper also pretended not to notice the man engrossed in the hatchling's skull yet decided to be cleaver and communicate to the man in an attempt to startle him. "Welcome to my humble place of business, my very old friend and beloved teacher," said the skull in a very much toned-down Scottish nuance. Pirah smiled and chuckled at the skull in the jar that looked right at him as he placed it back on the shelf where he found it.

"You were expecting me, yes?" answered Pirah, who now looked toward the man behind the counter, returning the look yet with a slight smile on his face.

"Indeed, my lord Pirah, for the very air doth fill my nostrils with the foul doings of the accursed and his minions."

"How fare thee, my dear friend?" asked Pirah as the two embraced. Long had it been since the two of them had seen each other, yet it was, too, as if only yesterday and nothing had changed but the surroundings of the times.

"I am as any sorcerer would be having these eight thousand years on the face of this Earth Mother. Yet I suppose being once mortal, I should be grateful for the time." They both laughed at the notion, seeing how there were very few immortals that had been mortal at one time. Merlyn offered a chair to Pirah, and they both sat down. With slight gesture of his finger, Merlyn locked the front door and flipped the Open sign to Closed, for he and Pirah would need to talk about these times without interruption. The historic sorcerer sat in silence while Pirah collected his thoughts about his task.

"Your face speaks volumes, my lord. Perhaps I should merely ask what it is that perplexes you?"

Pirah smiled then spoke. "I must go to Asgard and speak with the All Father with the intention of bringing the Norse Gods into the inevitable fray that is coming ever closer, my lord Merlyn, and so what I have come to ask is this: what know you of the disposition of Odin, Frigg, and all of the Aesir?"

Merlyn looked back at Pirah for but a moment then chuckled. "So sure you are, my lord, that I have been so close to the Norse Gods and I would have that information?"

Pirah did not hesitate. "Yes."

"Oh well, then you would be right in your assumption, my lord. As it happens, yes, I have been close to the All Father, and he has been quite displeased with mortal kind for some six thousand years now. I do believe." Pirah simply smiled and decided that having a meal and some ale would be the thing to do at this time, for he would be in long conversation with his old friend, and not all about the Gods of the Norsemen but of things that had happened since the time of his leaving the realm of Mystics and living as a Mortal, which then provoked the spell of forgetting. Pirah mentioned a good restaurant that would provide the required setting and repast; they both nodded and then vanished.

Quainor stepped from the portal he had created and stood in what would be called a pristine picture of what was once the North American continent as it was before the time of humans. It seemed superimposed and ever changing to the whim of the thoughts of the Spirits that dwelled in this part of the Mystic realm. He could look to any direction and see the various Spirit Gods' impression of how they would show the Mortals how they should live upon the face of Earth Mother, in harmony and reverence to the Spirits of the land. Long ago did Pirah send Quainor, the steward to this place, to learn and master his art as one who would hold domain over that which grows. He stood looking, feeling, reaching out to what could not be seen. He then spoke.

"I feel you here, and you know why I have come. Now I ask you come forth so we may see each other and hold council on this thing."

A voice spoke in the ancient language of the first people. "We cannot see you as you are. You must let us see you." Quainor looked about himself and shook his head; with a gesture of his left hand, he changed his appearance to a native of the lands that these Spirits were steward to. His face bore the paint of a shaman, along with the cloak made of the hide of a white bison. His head was adorned with a band around it sporting two owl tail feathers, with the tail of a fox falling over his shoulder. Around his neck was a necklace of cougar fangs and a medicine pouch. His trousers were changed to leggings, topped with a soft buckskin codpiece. He had in his left hand a staff of wood with the horns of a bison on the end, decorated with the flight feathers of a raven, and in his right hand a branch of sage.

The voice spoke once more. "We see you now, Ptsaysanwee, once a student now the Shaman."

Quainor placed the sage branch over his heart and spoke. "You honor me, great creator of the land of the first people. Now I must see you." Clouds began to gather in the sky toward the horizon, with beams of sunlight blazing between them as the sound of voices from thousands of years called forth these Spirit Gods through the ages of humans on the face of Earth Mother. The voices grew ever higher and louder as that of chanting by the other Spirits that were still unseen. The clouds then parted just at the horizon, where a figure could be seen approaching on horseback—a magnificent site of a young man, a warrior of the plain's tribes, his face and body painted in the fashion of a war chief, carrying a lance and shield with a knife at his side, a quiver of arrows on his back as well as a horned bow and his steed painted for war as well.

The man on horseback seemed to come ever closer to Quainor, now Ptsaysanwee, with each stride of the horse, yet he was far away at first. In just moments, the young rider was only a few paces from the Mystic from Avalon. With an intense fire in his eyes yet an undaunted face, the warrior spoke. "Come, Ptsaysanwee. We must sit and smoke and gather the others about the fire. For there is much to talk about."

Quainor looked up at the man and said, "Yes, Wakan-Tanka. There is much."

In another part of the realm of Mystics, a place that would seem so far from Quainor yet so very close to Avalon, stood Pirah, alone yet not without purpose and the resolve he had set out with. The old one stood in what had been called the roots of Yggdrasil, the foundation of the nine worlds that made up the Norse universe. He waited for the herald that was soon to come, for his presence there would not go unnoticed by the Aesir, for Pirah himself was there from the beginning—before time, before everything.

The sound of the hooves approaching from a mist that had rolled in gave Pirah some anticipation of an acknowledgment that the All Father and his court would grant him an audience or bid him to leave and never return. If the latter were the case, Pirah could only hope that the Gods of Asgard would remain neutral in the coming fray, for if they had sided with the accursed, then the battles would become ever more devastating.

The Norse Gods did not give quarter, nor did they ask for any. The mist parted, and a tall woman with long flowing blond hair that reached her thighs sat upon a great steed with hide, mane, and tail matching her own tresses. She wore a full-length gown that had intricate stitching and embroideries of Nordic runes about the seams and hems. The cloth itself left little to the imagination, for it was sheer enough to see the fullness of her hips, the tautness of her middle, and her large yet firm breasts that protruded through her hair.

Behind her the image was repeated by two other women mounted on black steeds of the same size, with long mane and tail, and yet the hair of these two was crimson as blood, their eyes blue as sapphires, and their skin pale and beautiful as the blond that preceded them. Pirah drank in the moment, for it had truly been an age since he had been greeted so by the Aesir. The woman walked their mounts to within arm's reach of Pirah, and as one they all bowed to the first. He returned the greeting with a deep bow of his own, showing deference to the lovely heralds of the Norse Gods. The blond spoke.

"We bid thee welcome, Lord Pirah, the old one in the name of the All Father, Odin, and our Lady Frigg."

"I am overwhelmed by the beauty of the delivery of this welcome," said Pirah. A fourth steed without rider appeared from the mist as black as what the two crimson-haired women were mounted on, and one the three purveyors of their master's message spoke.

"Please accept this gift, my lord, and follow us to the hall of the Aesir, where the All Father waits." Pirah climbed to the saddle of the beautiful horse, and all four turned and strode into the mist. No sooner did they enter the shroud of fog than they emerged in what was thought of as Asgard to the Mortal storytellers of the fifth age of humans. The four riders continued along a path that seemed to make its way as they rode upon it and then discontinued behind them. The beautiful maids paid no mind, only looking forward, as did Pirah, for this magic was not new to him.

The path began to ascend to what looked as a very long wooden building, quite tall and magnificent to behold; each board and metal inlay was carved with the runes of the Norse Gods that dated back to the time of the first and his role in the foundation of bringing forth the All Father and the others who became the Aesir. The blond maid raised her hands, then spread them wide. As she did so, the great doors of the building opened to reveal an immense hall with a long table lined with benches and high-backed wooden chairs, all covered with the same carvings of runes with heads of Dragons and great serpents as well.

There was only one person in the great hall, a man of the same stature as Pirah. He stood at the other end of the long table, his visage covered by a full-length cloak with the hood over his head, covering his face except for the long beard with braided moustache and silver rings throughout. Pirah dismounted and bowed graciously to the three maidens of the great hall of the Aesir, who did herald the All Father's welcome. The three bowed and turned their mounts as one, yet the fourth mount stayed and meandered about, grazing on sweet grass that grew just outside the huge doors. The man motioned for Pirah to enter the hall and walked toward him as he did. When he came close enough to be seen under his hood, the man turned and stepped toward a chest on the floor just inside the entrance. He knelt down before the chest and opened it. Reaching in, he brought out a bundle of clothes, a pair of soft leather boots, and a helm of polished steel and silver with a bejeweled band about the noseguard and head. He placed the articles on top of the chest and stood while examining Pirah from head to toe with a wave of his hand. He then opened a tall cabinet just next to the chest and withdrew a great broadsword sheathed in a magnificent hard hand-carved leather scabbard, the handle and pommel both equally magnificent with hand-wrapped leather and polished silver. Lastly, he produced from the cabinet a dagger with carved handle and double-edged blade with yet again hard leather scabbard.

He then placed the articles he produced at the feet of Pirah and spoke. "Will you allow me to wash your pained and troubled feet, Lord Pirah of old?" The man produced a large bowl of water and cloth while silently a young paige set a stool behind Pirah and motioned for him to sit. Pirah looked at the man and said yes as he seated himself. After the man had finished washing Pirah's feet, he then spoke one again. "Welcome to the hall of the Aesir, old one. It has been long, and you have been missed."

Pirah stood as the man did raise himself as well. The man pulled back his hood, revealing a full lustrous head of gray hair, a leather patch sewn to his right eye socket, and a questioning flare of his left. Pirah took the man by his shoulders, looked him in that eye, and said, "The fault is mine, Odin, king of Asgard, All Father to the Norsemen, and lord over the Aesir, and I have come for answers to questions as well as to ask for forgiveness." Odin shook his head and chuckled.

Feckulis stood in the middle of the circle of Gods that made up the ancient diocese of Greek Gods who reigned supreme over the Eastern European and Middle Eastern realms of the Aegean Sea, rivaled only by the fods of Egypt and the lands conquered by the pharaohs. The circle in question was the very heart and soul of the Gods of some amazing tales of glory and adventure brought to life by poets and singers of songs that beheld the beauty and mystery that was Olympus.

Bah Di Ah Aziza stood next to him as both of them looked up at the God of Gods in this realm, who took great pleasure in making himself larger than any man and insisted that the other Gods do the same when addressing "other than Gods" in issues of great consequence, such as it was at this moment. Zeus sat on his polished marble throne with an almost imperceptible leer on his face as he assessed the tall beauty from Avalon. Bah Di Ah met his gaze only with a purposeful look of sincere necessity. To the mighty Zeus's left was the ever jealous and vengeful Hera, who would not hesitate to make the lives of the two from Avalon and the entourage that came with them a continuous nightmare if she were to even suspect her husband having his way with the tall and ever so beautiful Lady Bah Di Ah.

"Wise was the thinking of the old one to send such capable and pleasing emissary to treat with me and the rest of the circle of Gods."

"Ever so wise is my beloved Pirah, oh mighty and eternal Zeus. May I also express my awe and admiration to Lady Hera, for your beauty is without challenge and therefore second to none," said Bah Di Ah. Feckulis tried to stifle his reaction to this ingratiating exchange, having once been under the scrutiny of Avalon and needing to wiggle his way out of a disastrous situation. He felt this moment quite humorous; Bah Di Ah, however, did not, and as she made a well-placed elbow to his ear as she ceremoniously motioned to Hera, Feckulis righted himself.

"Let us be quite clear, Lady Bah Di Ah. We are intimately aware of the goings-on about the world as of late, and by late, we mean for the last five decades of humans—no more than a blink of an eye for any of the Gods. Yet in that time, the accursed has beset his forces, most of which are clandestine in nature and are ready to deliver a hammer stroke to all life on the face of Earth Mother. We have been cast aside by the followers of the Nazarene, though his teaching had been butchered by humans to their manipulations and deeds of corruption," spoke Zeus.

Hermes spoke. "Behold, my lady. What would be to the benefit of the Gods of Olympus to bring forth our powers and legendary heroes to this fray? Will the Gods be honored as before?"

"This is a question we all have," said Apollo.

Bah Di Ah stood quietly, not having quite the answer these Gods of great power and knowledge wanted. Then Feckulis spoke. "Please forgive this unworthy Mystic, great and omnipotent beings of Olympus, but may I have a moment to share some insights with you?" A quizzical look formed on Bah Di Ah's face; as she looked down at Feckulis, he returned with his own look of "Trust me."

"Very well, Feckulis? Is it? We shall hear what you have to say. Be very particular and use what wisdom you have in your words, wizard, or you may find yourself at the mercy of the Gods," said Zeus.

Feckulis took a deep breath and began. "I speak to all of you, the deities of old and on behalf of the powerful and beloved of Avalon as well, as the Mystic realm in which we all dwell. This terror that besieges us is indeed real and about to happen, and those that stand by idly will either be relieved if the victory is for the good of all or suffer their own war of survival if the accursed has his way—and his way is not total victory but the continuous chaos and mayhem that is his way. At this very moment, all about the realms of Mystics, Spirits, and Gods, those of Avalon are holding this same council to find out where they stand if allowed.

"I believe this, oh mighty Gods of Olympus. There will be no denying of any Wizards, Mystics, Spirits, Demons, or Gods once this is made manifest. The age of man that is now will never again be the way of complicity that is the norm of today." Feckulis looked to each of the Gods of Olympus, meeting their gaze equally, for he was all too aware of the eternal mayhem that would be his former master's compulsion and lustful desire.

The Gods of the circle looked about to see what the others were thinking or perhaps communicating telepathically. Bah Di Ah spoke. "Great ones, my lord Feckulis speaks the truth, for we have felt the carnage of what he speaks within the very walls of Avalon and the realm of Ogres with the demise of mighty Hymmnaught, an attack on the Dragon realms Argain and Eschrokahn Veh, as well as a skirmish in the land of the Yeti on the face of Earth Mother. The horror has begun." Zeus looked about and then met the gaze of Hera, who gave the slightest nod to the ruler of the Gods; he then looked to the empty chair on farthest side of the circle from him—at one time not a conspicuous thing but now ever so troubling as it was the chair of his brother, who never missed an opportunity to thwart, defy, cause mischief, and generally anger Great Zeus, the God of the Underworld, Hades.

Zeus looked to his other sibling Poseidon and spoke. "I believe we are committed whether the desire strikes or not, brother. I may command you to open the gates of your realm to flood the Underworld, for there are many held in that dark place that would serve the accursed for vengeance alone."

Poseidon nodded in agreement, though troubled was his face, and so he spoke. "Brother, he is the oldest of us, and though he is troublesome, he is still of our line. Could we not once again reason with Hades?"

"Try if you wish, brother, but I think it for naught. He has wanted just this thing with just such an ally to give him the power he would need. If you do go the Underworld to hold council with our brother, I would beseech you to gather those from him that would fight for Olympus. You know of whom I speak," answered Zeus.

"Look no further, mighty Zeus, for those gifted with the blood of the Gods have broken the bonds of the Underworld, and we are here." From outside the circle of the Gods came a dynamic voice as well as the footfalls of several men, or Demigods as it were. They came boldly and with purpose into the circle, each looking as though having just left a great battle, covered in soot and blood, with wounds that were nearly healed, for their immortal bodies possessed that ability to an extent.

"Greetings, Achilles, Hercules, and all of you," said Hera. The group bowed as one then rose as Hera motioned. "Then it is settled. Go with the Avalon to hold council, and make ready to join what is in motion, and send me word of what is in the making. Hermes will go with you," commanded Zeus, highest of the Gods of the Acropolis.

Hercules paused for a moment then spoke. "Forgive me, Father, but we have another." The Gods looked quizzically at Hercules as he motioned toward the entrance to the semicircle where the Gods met.

There was the sound of a chain, a very light chain, and the panting of a beast—not just one but three. A small girl with black hair and large gray eyes, holding a slight chain that had a strange glow to it, appeared and was followed by none other than the guardian of the gates of the Underworld, Cerberus, with said chain attached to all three of the collars around the necks that carried all three of his heads. The three-headed hound stood nearly ten feet tall and didn't seem to mind his situation at all. The girl who held the chain simply looked about the circle at the Gods, who almost couldn't believe what they saw. The question being, how did the keeper of Cerberus abscond with Hades's beloved pet without a scratch?

"Dear Gods and Goddesses of Olympus, I give you Oraiell, keeper of Cerberus, the guardian of the gates of the Underworld and the dreaded three-headed hound himself, come to join the battles to come," said Hercules.

CHAPTER 7

Ogres, Celoth, Vessiel's Wrath

Orokoth stood at the window of his chamber, looking intently to the forest and hills that was just half a league from the walls of his castle, which served as the seat of power in the realm that was Celoth. The air was chilled, and it raised his skin, giving him a slight shiver as he did not cover his nudity. The woman that still lay in his bed, also not covered, rested her head on her hands and elbows, gazing at the half giant that she only minutes ago was engaged in fierce and ongoing carnal pleasure with. Orokoth turned and looked at the woman; she was nearly as large as he was and quite sturdy, as most Celoth woman were, with blond hair and dark eyes, her breasts protruding at her sides as she lay on her belly with, her firm round buttocks glistening with perspiration from the pounding they received.

What an amazing gift this woman had with oral abilities and knowledge of pleasures. He wondered why he hadn't had her before. His mind was occupied at the moment with the fact that nearly one and a half million troops were closing in on his castle, and every stronghold and village between his borders and the gates of his walls had been completely laid waste by those troops. He had, however, gathered his own armies to his keep and fortified the outlying areas, creating kill zones for his archers and trebuchet. He prepared for siege with no knowledge of how long it would be or if his lands would survive, for this time it was not the Wizards that were coming. It was Growgothal. Vessiel, their queen, was angry and determined to erase Celoth from existence and recorded history. There was no way to foresee what bounds she would cross in her quest to avenge her beloved Hymmnaught.

He decided that he would deal with it as it came, and one thing was certain—he would receive no help from Favlos, the deceiver, or any of his allies, not even Algala, who also enjoyed his endowment not but a week earlier. Amirchesch had fled with his Dragon riders to parts unknown in the Mystic realm and had not been heard from. Perhaps if he could find some rouge Mystic and bribe him to open a portal to the realm of Mortals or escape to Avalon, he could persuade those in league with the old one to spare his lands by convincing Vessiel to stay her hand. He chuckled; best to make the best of things, he decided. Orokoth looked at the half-giant wench on his bed and felt his cock grow hard. She, in turn, lifted herself up onto her knees then back on her ass, resting on her heels, spreading her knees wide, with her hands stretched out, palms up, ready to begin again.

He put himself closer so she may take his now fully engorged cock in her hands, then bowing her head down to take him in her mouth, she began to lick and suck with moaning sounds coming from her throat. She cradled his testicles in her hand and gently rubbed them while stroking his shaft rhythmically, allowing her tongue to slide out of her mouth, licking his head and area just below it. "Gods!" he gasped as almost immediately he felt his climax about to erupt, only to be brought back down to mere pleasure. She pulled his cock from her mouth then spun around, offering him her backside, and he wasted no time. He worked his cock into her anus, and she let out a groan, for she seemed to enjoy this more than anything. He started thrusting back and forth with gusto, and she cried out in absolute orgasmic bliss, which encouraged him to thrust even harder.

To his surprise, she clinched onto him, causing the sensation to escalate to the point of a volcanic climax for the both of them. He collapsed almost immediately just to one side of her, both of them gasping for air, their hearts pounding yet slowing down, giving them a moment to catch their breath. "Tell me again. What is your name, my sweet?"

The wench looked at him with a mischievous grin and said, "Names at this time, my lord, are not very important, only the moment." She wiped a drop of perspiration from his forehead that was about to enter his eye.

"Very well, yes, I can see your point, as my lands are about to engage in a battle that may or may not go the way I've planned," said Orokoth.

"No, my lord." She rose to her knees once again and bid him to rise with her, making him believe she was going to continue the sexual revelry, and as she leaned into him for a kiss, she lifted his chin ever so slightly and brought her fist from behind her back with such speed and power that it smashed his teeth, jawbone, and nose, sending him from the bed and sliding across the floor, crashing into the wall on the other side of the room.

Around her neck was an amulet with an oblong jewel in the center. As he lay on the floor, stunned and near unconscious, trying to get up, he looked and could not believe what he was seeing. The women grabbed the amulet and broke the chain it hung from, which began a transformation from the wench he just sodomized, to his worst nightmare. He couldn't get himself up, for the blow he took was incredibly powerful. No Celoth woman could hit that hard, and as the transformation took shape, he understood too well how she could do so. "I've never had a Celoth half-giant bastard before. Perhaps I should let one or two live just for my own enjoyment, perhaps more," came a voice from the now complete being that was once the Celoth wench.

Orokoth spit and cursed. *"Cunt!"* The being strode toward him, not showing any concern about her nudity or if any guards were alerted. She walked ever so deliberately toward him until she stood over him, and then she knelt closely and smiled.

Vessiel looked the Celoth brute in the eye and let her long Ogress tongue emerge from her mouth and lick the blood from his face, causing him to wince in pain. Her breasts were close enough for him to feel the heat coming off her, and he could taste her scent in his throat. She spoke once again. "I gift your last fuck, your last climax, from your cock that

I did suck. In my ass you did come. Explode you did like a bursting ripe plum, but now it's time that I collect, for the tally you took was of a terrible sum." She took hold of his giant head in both hands, hands that nearly covered both sides of his face, and she pressed ever so tightly, and he began to scream in pain from his wounded face being gripped. She then ever so quickly twisted his head from left to right, and his screaming stopped then again and once more; his head came free from his giant shoulders with a sickening ripping sound of sinew and skin. She held the head of Orokoth by the hair and stared in his eyes as the life that was left seeped away, bleeding from his torn neck. She spoke in the Ogre tongue. "I will give you this. You're not bad as a grudge fuck."

Vessiel retrieved the amulet and walked over to the same window where Orokoth stood. She then held the oblong jewel so as to be seen clearly, then in her other hand held up the head of Orokoth. The jewel emitted a soft glow that could only be seen by one who possessed the correct eyeglass. Bosurous held the glass to his eye and confirmed that his queen was still alive and had achieved the first part of her vengeance. He then looked to General Tarlus and said, "It is done." Tarlus looked up and behind into the great eye of the Argain messenger, sent to find out the intentions of Queen Vessiel of Growgothal.

"Go to the old one and the Avalon lady Rhona with the message you were handed, but if you would, retrieve my queen, lest she find herself captive by the Celoth naked and banded."

"At once, my lord general." The he and his escort took flight, headed toward the castle of Orokoth, now Dead. With just a few strokes of their wings, they were within the walls of the keep, found the window Vessiel was standing in, lightly picked her up, and shot back to the skies before any alarm or action was taken. Too late, the guards heard the beating of wings making haste. The Argain returned to where Bosurous and Tarlus stood and gently placed Vessiel before them then took to skies.

The two Ogres dropped to one knee before their queen, and Tarlus spoke. "Shall we begin, Your Grace?"

She held up the severed head, looking at the shocked expression on the face of her dead enemy, and said, "Yes, my lord General, let us begin."

Tarlus moved to the edge of an outcropping that overlooked a vast plain where the mass multitudes of warriors had been arranged with trebuchet and ballista as well as battering rams and various siege engines.

He walked over to a brazier with hot coals and lit a torch, held it over his head, and waved it three times. There was the sound of horns blasting out their commands, followed by an ominous roar of Ogres seething in their bloodlust. The mass began to move toward the castle of Orokoth and form lines of shields and spears. The trebuchet and ballista rolled along for some distance until placed in position for bombardment, and all the while, the defenders of the castle stood watching and waiting for commands that did not come. The tension began to grow ever more as the Ogres drew closer, all the while chanting in unison every stride in their advance.

The Celoth commander at the wall of the castle looked to his subordinates and said, "Where is Lord Orokoth?"

Then before an answer was given there was a shout, "Take cover!" as a barrage of flaming projectiles came flying through the morning skies. The Ogres had begun their barrage with a vengeance, hurling both immense boulders and flaming pods full of incendiary particles that would burst and spread their burning death and destruction into the ranks of the Celoth and within the castle walls. The defenders held fast, for hey had had many encounters through their time as soldiers, and this particular battle would define whether they were going to survive as a form of life.

Vessiel had no intention of letting that happen. From behind the walls, the sounds of shouting commanders and troops assembling could be heard by those just outside. The Celoth commander gave the order *"Open fire!"* The trebuchet within the walls hurled their own version of death at the Ogres in an attempt to cut down the numbers that seem to go on beyond sight. At the sight of the return fire, the Ogres picked up their pace from a march to rapid jog though still keeping cadence; the jog became faster until it became a full stride charge, and the chant became a full-throated roar with bloodcurdling screams. The charge at first resembled a mad, headlong avalanche of spears, axes, and shields, but as the mass grew closer, they split, creating a deep V shape with two sharp points at the vanguard, yet at the crook of the formation, there was a condensed position of full-length shields locked together yet keeping pace. The Celoth had not seen this formation before, yet some counter had to be employed; the commander barked orders to form a shield wall, and the tropes obeyed, locking together their own shields with spears protruding. The Ogres pressed on, still closing the gap between them and the Celoth.

As the two points of the Ogre formation were just about to clash with the shield wall of their enemy, the locked shields of the Ogres in the crook opened, and what came out made the blood of the Celoth run cold.

Screaming with nothing but bloodletting in their eyes came the most hideous and frightening sight beheld by anyone in the Mystic realm. These beings were called the Verrace, conjured many ages ago by the warring factions of old to bring horror to the Mystic kings, that they would submit without so much as drawing a sword, for they were not only devastating but nearly impossible to kill. These abominations had been kept in secret by mercenary lords that charged heavy payment for their use. They were hidden in various mountain cave dwellings, mostly in the border lands of other realms for quick deployment until called upon for paid service. Pirah himself had forbidden their use, for they had a propensity to breed unchecked, and thus control of them would be lost, and an infestation would be inevitable.

Vessiel had no qualms about using whatever she needed to avenge her beloved, even if there were consequences. However, she knew once the Verrace had their way with the Celoth, they would have to be called to stand down or perhaps even be dispatched; General Tarlus had made provisions for just this possibility—or perhaps inevitability. The Celoth commander upon the wall was no stranger to these foul creatures and was not about to be decimated by them. He had ideas of his own in the maters of being under siege, and so he looked to his subordinates and uttered, "Let them wade through the pit." The lower ranks bowed and went about giving the commands set forth by their lord general. The Verrace charged screaming and howling at the Celoth line, crashing into them, throwing their bodies against the shields while the solders on the other side thrust back with spears and swords that would gash and puncture but seemed to only enrage the beasts.

The only ones that fell were those that were decapitated, and even then, the head lived on temporarily. The Ogres smashed into the Celoth ranks and, in true Ogre fashion, fought with their enemy with brutality and vengeance for their queen. The Celoth did fight back, for their very existence was at stake. Even Vessiel could appreciate the showing of the half giants on the field of battle. This time, however, there would be no egress and no cover from Borians, for nearly the entire Celoth nation in this campaign had been annihilated for the most part, and stragglers were being hunted. The castle of Orokoth had been surrounded and cut off; even Lady Algala had turned from this fight; though she could have rescued Orokoth and a good deal of his armies, the endeavor bore no profit for her.

Horns sounded from the walls of the castle, and the center of the shield wall stepped back in a methodical gait as the Verrace continued to thrust forward into the Celoth lines. Tarlus saw this and spat his observation to the mercenary commander. "Your monsters need retreat at best, or they will be destroyed by your stupidity is my only guess." The commander growled then waved a hand to his men on the field, who did not pay him any notice for they were too engrossed with what they thought was a breach of the Celoth lines; in reality they were playing right into the hands of their alleged prey.

At a point where the Celoth formation seemed to be near collapse, the gates of the castle opened, and the shield wall fell back from side to side, where there was but a token formation that also fell back as the Verrace stormed through the gates, charging headlong into what seemed to be a huge palisade with Celoth backed against the buildings. The ruse was complete; the bloodthirsty mass charged into the empty area, and as the last of them poured through the gates, the trap was sprung. With almost imperceptible swiftness, the beams that supported the false ground about them disengaged, and the lion's share of the palisade collapsed beneath them.

The contingent of Verrace found themselves in a pit with no escape, screaming and slashing at one another, trying to get out. Unfortunately, this was not the end of the trap by any means. The farthest end of the pit had several round openings as the end of a pipe would be, measuring a little more than a foot in diameter; there was a sound of rushing fluid coming from the pipes that caught the attention of the Verrace, and they became silent. The viscous fluid shot from the opening with great pressure, striking the foul creatures and dashing them to the floor of the pit that was their undoing, for the substance that it was dissolved flesh and bone and other living matter, and the Verrace screamed out in rage that changed to agony then inevitable silence.

This caused the Celoth within the walls to cheer for winning the moment, yet the battle was not over, not by a great deal. The people inside the castle began filling in the pit with stones and earth; at the same time, the reserve warriors poured through the open gate to reinforce the ranks already engaged with Ogres, in once again a blow-for-blow exchange, as did happen at the gates of the Ogre capital. "The keep of Hymmnaught, king of Growgothal," Tarlus growled in the Ogre tongue. "A fucking waste of coin for those maggot-ridden shits. Leave my sight, commander of nothing, or you'll join your useless hoard in their demise," he told the mercenary leader.

"I do not understand the Ogres' speech, my lord general. What is thy bidding?"

Tarlus turned to the scowling mercenary and spoke. "Pity is what there should be for someone as foolish as you." He then grabbed him by the throat and lifted him above his own head with no effort and tore the bag of gold from his belt, tossing it to the ground. The commander of the Verrace tried to pry the fingers of Tarlus from his throat, but he may as well have clutched at stone. Tarlus walked over to the edge of the outcropping, where Vessiel himself and his subordinates watched the battle below and deftly flung him out into empty space without interest in his flight. "Find the rest of his ilk, and give them the same choice. Let it be known not to displease our queen—or me."

Tarlus then addressed Vessiel, who had been watching the whole battle while bathing and being dressed by her ladies-in-waiting, five Ogress women of similar dimension and beauty (for Ogres). "Shall I deliver the hammer stroke, Your Grace?" Vessiel simply nodded and continued to watch the battle below. Tarlus then gave orders to his subordinate generals, and signals were raised to be seen by the commanders of the reserves. Nearly seven hundred thousand Ogres surged from the rear areas while in formation toward the castle of the now dead Orokoth of Celoth. The fresh troops encircled the Celoth, battling with the first wave and closing in—no shield wall, no sounding of horns, simply unbridled carnage. Vessiel's revenge was nearly complete; the next and final step was to pull down the castle leaving no stone standing. This would be done by Bosurous, the Ogre Mystic.

The overwhelmed Celoth fell back once again into the castle but could not close the gates as the Ogres pressed their attack; the pit that once served them well was no longer an option, and the battle was now being fought in the courtyard as Celoth and Ogre clashed and fell, covering the ground with the blood of both factions. The intensity of the fighting grew as the Celoth would not go quietly to their extinction, even rallying several times, pushing back the Ogres toward the gates, only to have more pour through and regain the lost ground. Far up in the castle, a subordinate officer and several of his men burst into the quarters of Orokoth and found the beheaded body of their lord sitting upright as Vessiel had left him. The shocked half giants stared in disbelief at the lifeless body of the once mighty ruler of Celoth, but the officer regained his faculties and barked orders to tell the lord general on the wall what had happened. The solders made haste as this might very well be the last order they would carry out before death or escape, but to what end? The officer then knelt next to the body of Orokoth and took up his right hand, which had his cygnet ring, and removed it, tucking it into his tunic. He then left the chamber with one last look at his now dead lord, wheeling about and making his exit—in the opposite direction that his men went. As the battle moved farther into the castle, the Celoth began to feather out and look for ways to escape, and though some did succeed in avoiding the onslaught, they were cut off by contingents placed outside the farther walls away from the initial attack.

However, there were other methods of escape, and the higher-placed Celoth lords and their retainers capitalized on these. They made hasty escape through tunnels that led far away for the castle with openings that were well hidden from sight by purposely overgrown foliage. Some were successful; others were not as they emerged among patrolling Ogres and found themselves fighting for their lives. While a group of Celoth were being forced to kneel just before being beheaded, a sergeant approached with a squad of Ogres and bellowed, "Not all of them. Save the prettiest for the pleasure of our queen. The order was just given. It appears she has developed an appetite for half giants that has been aroused somewhat."

The young and strong were singled out and put in irons while the others met their fate immediately after, and as the finishing of Vessiel's vengeance came to pass, Bosurous came forth and made gestures with his hands that produced fluctuations in the air about the battlefield and castle, causing the walls to crack and crumble. With a great roar, debris fell and structures crashed as the castle of Orokoth laid waste before all who were there to see. Vessiel stood looking at what her forces had brought upon her enemy and gently sipped her goblet of wine. "Let my armies feast and fuck to their heart's content, for they have earned their queen's gratitude. Once they have had their revelry, we march to Avalon and fulfill my husband's oath," said Vessiel to Tarlus.

Tarlus then asked, "What of the succession to the throne, Your Grace?"

"When all is settled, my lord general."

Tarlus bowed to his queen, then turned and left her with her attendants. He then motioned for his aide to walk with him. "The queen will have festivities, and the tropes will as well. Let this go for ten days, then we march and join the Avalon, for I believe our fight continues to Corsolvess and the face of the Mortal realm, Earth Mother."

"As you command, Lord General," said the aide.

CHAPTER 8

Feckulis No More

The council of Avalon sat in a semicircle, having been summoned by Lord Pirah to hear the reports of the emissaries that had been sent to find out where the Gods of old stood on the now very real battle for which factions would inevitably rule the mystic and Mortal realms. Before them stood the emissaries that had been sent to the various gates of realms where the Gods chose to dwell and continue their omnipotence in the universe of the Greater Powers. Among these emissaries were Lords Quainor, Feckulis, Lady Bah Di Ah Aziza, and the old one himself, Pirah, along with some who had returned with them from these places that were revered in another time, in another age. Lady Rhona, at the very center of the semicircle, looked about and found herself pleased at the turnout of ancients that returned with those of Avalon. She held in her hand a rolled parchment that had been handed to her by the keeper of the left door of the great hall of Avalon. It simply read, "I go now to Merlyn and the Aesir," in Pirah's hand, and there he stood with three Valkyrie attending him and one God of the Aesir.

Bah Di Ah stood with Feckulis along with the heroes of old from Olympus who had returned with them from their quest. Unexpected but much appreciated were several representatives from the Hindi Gods of old that needed no emissary, for they had already had dealings with the forces of the accursed among their followers. Quainor stood alone yet somehow looked confident that his journey brought success, as well as others that had been sent about the realms of the old Gods from the different ages of life on Earth Mother. Lady Rhona motioned to call the gathering to order, but as she did, more Gods and representatives of Gods began to enter the great hall. Behind the semicircle were the Dragons Argain, Serous, Aralainious, having recovered from her battle wounds, and Lord Tarc, who had to allow the members of the court to climb about their limbs and neck to make room for the ever-increasing reception of envoys. As the room became almost full to capacity, Gloria, waif of the great hall of Avalon, spoke with an amazingly loud and commanding voice.

"Please take your places, all who have come to Avalon, be you God or Godling, lord, or squire, for we must get underway!" Many of those with power simply levitated to the higher levels of the great hall, giving room for others to spread out.

Apparently, the gathering of these envoys seemed to go on from the great hall to the palisade and out into the city of Avalon, for the Gods of old were many, and they wanted to know what was being done with this different affront being put upon the realms by Favlos, the accursed. Truly it was a new type of affront, for there seemed to be no ending, only a beginning, and no one could see when that occurred. As the hall went, silent Rhona spoke.

"Dear friends, thank you all for coming and for whatever the task you have been sent, whether it be to tell us your benefactor only wishes to be informed or you have come to tell us you've joined the fray that is now. Avalon bids you welcome. Now I would like to hear from Lord Pirah and what he would have for us from the Aesir."

Pirah stepped forward, and his escorts stepped with him until he was at the center of the semicircle. "I give you, my lady Rhona, Ull, son of Sif, stepson to Thor of the Aesir and Asgard." All in the room bowed, as did Rhona. Not to go unnoticed, the lady of the lake gave a quizzical nod to the three beautiful maids that were at this time strangers to her. Pirah then spoke. "These three ladies are my new attendants gifted to me by the All Father to serve as I would need. They are Luften, Frieda, and Brendi." Each girl bowed as her name was spoken in deference to Lady Rhona, who found it difficult not to be a little jealous of the three beautiful Viking women who now shared the attention of her beloved teacher.

Ull took one more step and spoke. "If it please my lady, the All Father, Odin, doth commission me to serve as liaison to the Aesir for Avalon and be at your bidding should you find my powers useful."

"I and the council are indebted to Odin of Asgard for his generosity and foresight," Rhona replied as Ull bowed and stepped back. Pirah and company stepped back from the semicircle, and as he turned, he met the gaze of Quainor, who seemed quite happy with his journey to the Spirit Gods of the southern and northern Americas.

"You missed your teachers, didn't you, my friend?" said Pirah.

"It was good, my lord, a successful and wondrous thing," Quainor replied. Bah Di Ah Aziza and Feckulis stepped forward to the center and bowed, followed by three others dressed in cloaks and linens of ancient Greece and a fourth wearing dark tight-fitting trousers and black shawl pulled over her head and face; she held in her hand a familiar, delicate chain that seemed to drag behind her and disappear.

"My lady, my lord Feckulis, and I bring you heroes of Olympus commissioned by Zeus himself, all once held in the Underworld by Hades, now free by their own hand."

Lady Rhona looked to Pirah; they both smiled and looked with regard at the hooded figure with the all-too-familiar chain in her hand. She stood just to the left of the center of the semicircle with little or no movement other than her cloak shifting as she regarded the others in the great hall of Avalon. "It is good to see you again, my beloved. Welcome home," said Pirah. All stopped their conversations and movements to focus on the hooded figure that garnered such attention from the old one, and yet none other seemed to know who this was save the Olympians. "Oraiell, it has been far too long. What have you there at the end of your chain?" Oraiell pulled back her hood and motioned in the direction of the center of the semicircle, and as though walking from some other room, into the next stroud, was the great hound that was Cerberus, guardian of the Underworld.

All in the room reacted with either gasps or sounds of praise, for this was truly a sight, as Cerberus had never left the gates that he had been placed at for eternity. "Forever bringing us surprises, my dear. I'm sure we will be hearing of this from Hades soon," said Lady Rhona. Badi Ah became perplexed at the familiarity between Pirah and Rhona, this dark, silent girl who seemed to be able to captivate with such ferocity. As if she could feel Badi Ah's thoughts, Oraiell stepped up to her, reached up to her hand, and gave it a gentle squeeze. This was a pleasant surprise to Bah Di Ah, for she had kept her distance since Olympus, but now she showed a different side to her persona.

"Now a new friend," said Rhona. Oraiell looked to Rhona and blinked to acknowledge her statement. The room was silent at last as the impact of Cerberus being brought in to the Great Hall was staggering, for the keepers did not challenge his entrance even though he had been cloaked. Others simply summarized that Bah Di Ah simply gave them the order to let the visitors pass as they would not have otherwise. Or perhaps they simply recognized the hooded figure and did nothing. At any rate, the hall had filled with Gods of old and heralds of such, and all wanted to state their case to the Avalon and those that called themselves friend and ally. Each of those that came was given time to speak, and not all were there to pledge fealty or commit the power of their being to this ongoing fight but only observe what unfolded in the coming engagements between the forces of the accursed and those of Avalon and the old one.

All had their own reasons to join in or not, for the world that they once knew had been transformed by deceivers and corrupters long ago, and many of the Gods had been simply cast aside by man. The discussions went on and on for several days, with many heated arguments and points taken, with even one of the factions mentioning that perhaps Pirah should simply urge Earth Mother to once again purge her surface of all life and begin anew.

This was not agreed on as a good portion of the assembly wished to regain their following in the mortal realm and take this age to a greater place. The gathering began to take the shape of other gatherings, with no resolve or forward movement, only an agreement that a plan or some change in conventional thinking must be employed, yet none seemed to come to any recourse. It was then that Achilles of the Olympians stood and called the attention of the assemblage of Gods and heralds.

"If you would so indulge me, my friends, I would like all to hear what I am to say, for I believe it has relevance to this gathering of ancient power and wisdom. You all have been told the stories of Greece and her heroes by the poets and scholars of every land on the face of Earth Mother, so I am certain you've all heard mine. It is that which you may want to revisit for it my own ways and my own vanity that brought my demise and sent me to the underworld from which my friends and I came to join this fight. For fighting is what we do best. We shall serve and serve well only if we all can come to an agreement, not soon, now." All looked about and kept silent, for the words of Achilles, though simple, were quite true. Once again, even with divine company, there were disagreements that came from pride and vanity. Feckulis walked up behind Achilles and touched his arm, and he wanted him to stand next to him as he addressed the room.

"Good patrons of this assembly, what mighty Achilles has said is true, and so it is urgent that we all make peace with our own egos and create a plan or—a nonplan—that will counter the intentions of the accursed Favlos. Other than great Pirah and beloved Lady Bah Di Ah Aziza, I myself am intimately aware of the ways of our enemy, and one thing is certain—that our discussions that keep us from coming to a resolve are exactly what he wants and has certainly planned on. I know this, for over the ages, I have been part of these incursions that failed, only this time, this time the approach has changed, and there will be no all-out battle—ever. We can seek out the strongholds and fight the incursions that unfold before us, but we shall never completely destroy our enemy. So I beseech all that are here and those that are watching by to conjure that we appoint our leader, take direction, and follow through with emphasis on knowing our adversary."

All were silent for the moment after Achilles and Feckulis spoke their truth to the assembly of Gods and their heralds in the great hall of Avalon. There was dead silence for a time until a hushed conversation was heard and others joined the small group, which became ever larger as those engaged seemed to agree with those that began the discussion. Pirah stood with a slight grin on his face, seeing that for once in a very long time, there was no shouting and posturing going on during such a discussion.

The group all seemed to be putting together their thoughts as to who would be such a leader, and so would they all fall in step with this ideal. One could hear a single voice say, "All in favor?"

The entire group replied "Aye." The group then spread out among those that were not in the center of the group to share the proposal. There was some grumbling with raised voices, but only for the moment as the suggested leader was a good one, and only the vain and pompous of them would argue that they themselves should be a better choice but were then convinced otherwise by those of greater wisdom and perhaps prettier flesh. The collective minds all acknowledged the one most logical choice and then turned their attention to the diocese of the Avalon council to state their conclusion. A single God of the Hindi spoke for the mass.

"Do we, the members of this assembly, have the undying love and dedication to Lord Pirah and all that call him friend and lord?"

Pirah bowed in acknowledgment, as did the Avalon council, the Argain, the black Dragons of Eschrokahn Veh, and all the other Mystic realm lords. "Then it will be as thus. We, the Gods and Spirit Gods of old, have declared that this encounter will require one of the Mystic realms that is not a God but indeed a leader, and one of magic just as is the accursed and his following, and so we have named Lady Rhona, our lady of the lake, as our sovereign and will follow her to whatever end this state of affairs becomes."

All turned to Lady Rhona and dropped to one knee, as did the same Hindi God. "Today until the end of these days shall we be at your service, with fealty and loyalty to our end if necessary, until the day come that we need not."

All stood as one exclaimed, "All hail Lady Rhona of Avalon!"

Rhona stood from her chair and spoke. "Mystics and deities, you all honor me with your faith and trust. I myself would have chosen another but for his wisdom and power."

Pirah interjected. "And did these great ones not choose you as you have learned to wield great power and have acquired your own wisdom, my lady?"

Rhona looked into Pirah's eyes, trying desperately to hold back her tears. "My teacher," she spoke as she bowed to the great Pirah, and so with that came great applause and the pounding of shields from the guardians that stood shoulder to shoulder in the great hall of Avalon. Once the accolades and applause died down and all had settled into their places again, Lady Rhona addressed the room. "I have something that I believe to be of great importance to Avalon and all that claim her as friend and ally. Lady Bah De Ah Aziza of Avalon and the Dragon realm Argain, will you do the honor?"

Bah Di Ah sidestepped next to Feckulis and extended her hand down to him; he looked up at her with an obvious "What is this?" about his face as he took her hand. She motioned that he walk with her to the center of the semicircle of chairs that formed the council of Avalon and then stood in front of him and dropped to one knee so she would be looking up at his still-stunned face.

She then spoke. "My new friend and ally to those of this assembly, we have all come together and have discussed an inconsistency in the realm of Avalon, and that would be your name. Your name that describes a state of foul and disgusting decay is no longer accurate to your being, and though your skills as assassin may be useful in the future, your name simply cannot be kept. The former name givers to you hold no sway here and therefore bear no credence. We of the Avalon have come together, as did my beloved teachers did once for me, and we offer you a new name—that is, Alduriil, lord of Avalon and Mystic to the realm."

Feckulis stood with watering eyes, looking into the equally watering eyes of Bah Di Ah then to the faces of Pirah, Rhona, Serous, and all the others of the council, and he dropped to one knee. "I, Alduriil, take this new name. With this I proclaim, Feckulis is no more."

CHAPTER 9

The Great Houses of Men

Quinstems, Wormskale, and Turkez stood before their self-proclaimed God king as he paid close attention to a small female human he had brought to him from the mortal realm—a comely lass that was just one head shorter than the average Dwarf woman yet well proportioned and not nearly as muscled. The three Lords of Corsolvess stood waiting with dour looks on their faces for a response from Favlos in regard to the next action to be taken in his ongoing war with the Mystic realm and the conquering and enslaving of Earth Mother.

"Are you quite sure we are ready for this?" asked Favlos, never taking his eyes from the little woman.

"At this time, Holiness, I believe we are quite ready to take this campaign to the realm of humans, as our insurgent progress has yielded many allies, both Mortal and Deity as well as the Monsters and Titans of old," Turkez replied.

Favlos looked up at Wormskale and asked, "What say you, Lord General? Are we ready for this mass attack upon the very being that is kept steward by my dullard counterpart Pirah?"

Wormskale shifted his weight in a manner depicting the approval of his king and placed his lower left hand on his sword pummel. With a quick glance at Quinstems, he said, "I do, Holiness, with the utmost confidence."

The self-anointed God king of Corsolvess never took his eyes off Wormskale as he spoke once again with a slightly menacing tone to his voice. "We pray that your 'confidence' is rooted in well-placed resources, my lord general, and not egotistical posturing. We are also waiting for some progress on another matter." Wormskale's poise seemed to deflate somewhat, much to the curiosity of Turkez and Quinstems. Both pretended that they didn't have knowledge of what exactly Favlos was speaking of.

Wormskale quickly gathered his thoughts and addressed his sovereign with more certainty than he was actually feeling. "Holiness, all is going as planned, and all will be placed at His Holiness's disposal in due time." Turkez and Quinstems exchanged glances with little expression, then returned their eyes to Favlos, who had lost interest in the conversation and was focused once again on the tiny mortal woman. With slight wave of his hand, he signaled to his high lords that they may leave and get on with their planning for the soon-to-happen strike on Earth Mother, but for now, he had better plans.

He motioned to the woman to remove her clothing, and with a come-hither grin on her face, she complied; with one pull of a string, her tiny gown fell to the throne room floor, revealing flawless porcelain skin, full round breasts that seemed to defy gravity, and yet more roundness in her hips, thighs, and the wondrous perfection of her derriere. Her toes and fingernails were painted black, as well as her lips, eyes, and hair. She then struck a seductive pose in front of her would-be host, not paying attention to the three who had yet to completely exit the throne room, stealing a final glance before passing through the entrance. She lightly stepped forward and straddled his left leg at the same time, unbuckling his trousers. "You don't seem to be uncomfortable in this place. Are you sure you're from a Mortal realm, my dear?" asked Favlos.

She smiled as she pulled his cock from his now wide-open and pulled-down garment and began to massage it. "I may have been this morning, Your Highness."

"Holiness will do," said Favlos.

"Holiness, but from what I have been seeing since I've been here, I'd have to say I'm from this realm from now on," she replied.

"An excellent outlook, my dear." Favlos let out a pleasurable noise as she slipped his now erect cock in her mouth and expertly went to work on it. Favlos thought to himself, "This one I'll keep."

As Quinstems, Turkez, and Wormskale left the throne room of Favlos, Lord Turkez mentioned to General Wormskale, "I certainly hope for your sake, Lord General, that whatever business you have with His Holiness that Lord Admiral and I are not privy to should be concluded with haste, for the time has come upon us that we launch or incursion on Earth Mother and the world of men."

Wormskale looked to Lord Turkez and Admiral Quinstems as they walked the halls and gave a growling huff. "Indeed," he replied, continuing down the hall until the three came to a crossing, where Wormskale took his leave of the other two.

Quinstems, in turn, went the other way to the right and proceeded down toward his chambers. Turkez, ever stoic, walked alone yet, for a moment, allowed himself the slightest bit of a smirk to appear on his face. Meanwhile, Wormskale reached his quarters in the castle of Favlos, where his subordinates waited for his orders. All snapped to attention when he walked in and dared not as much as blink until he gave his permission. He paced about the room while all stood facing different directions but not moving a single millimeter nor breathing, for they all knew that their commanding general was in a mood of the most foul and could quite possibly sever the head of the one most foolish to blink.

He stopped pacing and motioned with his lower left hand, giving them all clearance to relax. "What do any of have to report on the traitor, and when can I expect delivery of his head?"

All looked to General Arteous, the master of spies, to answer. Arteous looked at his commander with cool assurance and took a half step toward him, then spoke. "My lord, I have dispatched three assassins to eliminate the traitor and over a hundred spies to gather information of the construct beast that was sent to kill the first, and though locating Feckulis has not been a problem, it has been near impossible to strike. However, we are discovering movements by the old one that seem to be most interesting."

"Please, my lord, continue," said Wormskale.

"A shapeless one observed Pirah himself giving a message to one of the keepers of the great hall of Avalon and then opening a portal to what seemed to be Earth Mother from the look of the other end. However, the portal closed quite quickly. This would not be so important but for the fact that Lady Rhona and Lord Pirah had just held council privately, and both, with great haste, took to their tasks," Arteous explained.

Wormskale looked about the room and said, "I know there must be more. The looks on your faces give you up completely."

Arteous motioned to a lower subordinate though a general all the same. "General Crowlus, if you would?" said Arteous.

"My lord general, as you know, we cannot pierce the walls of the great hall of Avalon, nor can our spies gain entrance. However, I have been made privy to some other movements of the Avalon and her allies throughout the Mystic realm and the halls of the old Gods of men."

Wormskale motioned and spoke, "You have my attention, General."

"It would seem that envoys have been sent to the Gods of Olympus, Asgard, the Spirit Gods of the north and south continents, as well as the Hindi, the Nippon, and old Cathay, and quite possibly the Gods from the Mother of Man [Africa], to join in battling the forces we command on the face of Earth Mother." Wormskale knew about the engagement of the old one and his party in the Himalayan mountains as well as the efforts of Turkez to bring the Gods to their service. The efforts of Lord Turkez had not been brought up to the God king, for only few had given their answer, and those that did have been lesser Gods at best.

Action had to be taken at once, or the tide may well turn for the Avalon, and regaining the momentum his forces had taken would be nearly impossible, thus relegating the battles to the Mystic realm and the eventual destruction of what was Corsolvess. "Assemble the armies for deployment to the staging points upon the face of Earth Mother. We have no time. Send word to Quinstems to get his ships into position and prepare them to battle with navies that can destroy nations." He then turned to Arteous and Crowlus. "Good work, my lords. Speak nothing of this to anyone, not Turkez or Admiral Quinstems and especially the snake." The group of generals all bowed and left the chamber as Wormskale poured himself a tankard of ale and took a long draft. He then looked out the window that reached from the floor to the ceiling and said to himself, "Ready? Fuck me if I know."

Turkez sat at his desk, poring over a huge tomb that covered the history of those that sat on the throne of Corsolvess and how the inevitable end did come to pass. Some were defeated outright by forces of Mystic realm inhabitants; others were destroyed by Pirah himself in a great battle, exchanging devastating bursts of pure energy only after manipulating great manifestations created from the very rocks and trees and sometimes the very elements that lived in the seas. Turkez pondered what the outcome of this different kind of war would be. All three of the mighty lords that had sworn their allegiance had been either destroyed or had simply withdrawn from the fray. His God king had most likely seen them as fodder from the beginning and so paid no mind to the obvious.

He began to turn another page when a voice distracted him. "My lord Turkez, I hope I'm not disturbing you."

Turkez, looking up at the source of this voice, thought for a moment before he spoke. "Not at all, Lord Admiral. How can I help you?"

Quinstems stood in the doorway with one hand resting on his sword and one hand holding a cup of wine while the other two were folded together. He looked at Turkez and spoke. "Are you aware of the actions that have been taken since our meeting with His Holiness?" Turkez closed the tomb he was reading through and leaned back in his chair.

"Not as yet, my lord. However, if I were the lord high general in possession of sensitive information that could spell the downfall of Corsolvess and yet another rout of His Holiness's forces, I suppose I would act very quickly and muster the forces at my command, placing them in concealment about Earth Mother as well as the Mystic realm."

Quinstems nodded thoughtfully then added, "He sends word to me that the fleet shall be engaging the naval forces of the Mortals on the oceans covering Earth Mother as well. Does that fall into the wondrous strike-and-retreat method, or has there been a change in plans?"

Turkez simply looked at Quinstems for a moment, then lifted his left brow.

Far from that conversation, on the face of Earth Mother stood Alitius and his high generals surveying the area of what would be called the outer lying woodlands that overlooked Arlington and the Potomac River as well as Washington, DC. Along with Alitius stood Pirah himself, dressed in modern entirely black Mortal attire, with a silver chain around his neck that sported a small amulet with the skull of a dragon and several rings on his right and left hands. Alitius grinned and spoke, "I'm still not used to you looking so . . . Mortal."

Pirah chuckled. "Well, take heart, my friend. In due time, the world will have to become used to many different appearances." Pirah looked down at the city for a moment longer then said, "Almost time." Alitius signaled with a motion of his hand for his generals to withdraw.

They all took steps backward, some sinking into the ground others, blending with the trees, until all were no longer visible to the naked eye. As soon as the last was hidden, another rose from the ground and approached the two lords and bowed his head. Alitius spoke. "What news, Aisus?"

The general looked about then showed deference to Lord Pirah before he spoke.

"There are no signs of those that hold allegiance to the accursed or his agents, my lord, nor are there any Trolls or constructs detected—yet." The general finished then turned and blended to the trees. Pirah looked to Alitius and said, "It's time to go public, my friend."

"The day I've waited for—this entire age."

All had been put into place as the leaders of all the great houses of men would be alone in their chambers at different times all about Earth Mother. This would be the opportunity for Pirah to project his image and the image of his brethren to make these leaders aware of what was about to befall upon them and that they must consider the course of action that they would take in the days, months, years to come, for everything now known to be reality was about to change in unimaginable ways. He began with the president of the United States.

Baron Hanor Orbus, elected to the office of the president for his second term, was walking toward his office chamber to close out his schedule binder for the day and review what was on the books for tomorrow morning. Thus far in his interim as president, he was more than accustomed to crisis management, both foreign and domestic, receiving intelligence of terrorist activity, creating solutions to impossible situations brought on by hostile members of the opposing party that refused to accept that a Black man gifted with enormous intelligence and unstoppable vision was voted into office—not once but twice—and managed to keep a cool, calm demeanor as well as an air of class and articulate finesse matched by no previous incumbent of the White House.

He walked down the hall and was greeted by White House employees as well as staff members, who all seemed to be very at ease with this commander in chief. As he reached his quarters, the Marine guards at the door snapped to attention and saluted as he passed with an "As you were, fellas." The Marines resumed the "at ease" stance. He unbuttoned his jacket and took it off, laying it across one of the chairs that was placed in the middle of the room, and sat down at his desk. He opened his ledger and began to make check marks and footnotes on the pages before turning each page, and then he stopped; something was not right in his office. He looked around the room, and there in the corner was a large fern in a planter barrow of the likes that would be outside in the White House garden—not in his office. He looked at the plant for several seconds then pushed the intercom to his personal secretary's desk.

"Yes, Mr. President?" a voice came over the speaker.

"Did the first lady happen to drop by while I was out?"

"No, sir, there have been no visitors or appointments beginning at 13:00 until now. Is there a problem, sir?"

He looked around the room and could see nothing else but turned his gaze back to the mysterious plant in his quarters. "No, Gwen, no problems, alpha two."

"Thank you, Mr. President. Alpha two received." He stood up and pulled a cigarette out of his pocket as well as a Zippo lighter, and just before he lit it, a voice came from across the room.

"Aren't you supposed to be quitting those?"

The president's head snapped to the direction of the voice, and he was shocked at the sight he was beholding. His Zippo lighter fell from his hand, still burning at the wick as it dropped. Yet before it could hit the floor, it stopped in midair and rose back to the president's eye level, flipped closed, and remained floating in place. He couldn't take his eyes off the lighter as he was stunned beyond belief and felt his stomach begin to turn with the acceleration of his heart rate. Out of reflex more than knowledge, he snatched the lighter from its seemingly unnatural place and steadied himself, putting his hand on the corner of his desk. The president curled his finger under the decorative molding and pressed the concealed panic button.

The desired effect did not happen, no team of highly trained Secret Service agents bursting through several concealed doors with flash-bang grenades going off or the apprehending of this intruder that seemed to possess some kind of unearthly abilities. "You might want to release that button, Mr. President. It has been disabled, and you may want to have a seat as your blood pressure is climbing quite quickly." The president watched as his jacket lifted from the chair; he placed it on and neatly hung itself on a coat rack behind his desk, complete with hanger. He then saw the chair that it was on positioned itself across from his uninvited guest. "Please, Mr. President, I would feel terrible if you lost your balance and fell. Please have a seat, and I'll explain what you're experiencing."

President Orbus slowly walked over to the chair that had moved on its own, still clutching the Zippo lighter in his hand with a death grip. He sat down and looked the man in front of him up and down, trying to get an idea of who or what he was. The being in question sat in a fine leather chair not quite tucked all the way in the corner of the room; he sat up straight yet with a very comfortable demeanor, with one leg crossed over the other. His shoes, socks, trousers, and everything else he wore seemed to fit perfectly, with not a single flaw, and entirely in black but for his jewelry, being of polished silver—three rings on his right hand and two on his left and a single chain with an amulet of what looked like a skull of a fierce beast on it. His hair was long and black, pulled back into a ponytail, and his ears sported several piercings. His face seemed about middle-aged and without facial hair. His eyes were hidden by perfectly round sunglasses. He sat down in the chair and placed the Zippo on the arm, took a deep breath, and crossed his own legs.

The man gestured with his hand, poured whiskey for the president from across the room, then poured a second. "I hope you don't mind. I do have a fondness for spirits of the Mortal realm, and a touch now and then is such a treat." The president glanced at the two glasses as they were placed on a serving tray then brought across the room by, apparently, this man's will. Baron Orbus, as most humans went, was not a man encumbered with a lack of vision or disbelief; although he was finding it difficult to believe what was happening, he couldn't deny that it was and therefore shifted his thinking to engage and identify this man and what it was he was there for. "Before I get into who you are or what it is you want, I'll reason that you . . . are not human? Or as you say, Mortal? Which also stands to reason that you are not of this world, yes?"

The man grinned and nodded as his glass of whiskey placed itself in his hand. The president continued, "You say you enjoy 'spirits of the Mortal realm.' Does that mean there are other realms that humans are not aware of?" As he spoke, the other glass met his hand as well.

"To your health, Mr. President," the man toasted the commander in chief, and they both took a sip of their glasses. "To answer your question, Mr. President, yes, there are several realms other than this, all of which I am a part of. However, that is not the reason for my visit. You see, I am here to let you know that everything that you and the rest of Mortal kind has come to believe as—for lack of a better word—normal is about to change forever."

The president looked at the man, trying to pick up some sort of tell that he was running a game with the intent on assuming control over the US government, but there was nothing, no sign he was lying or even bending a half truth. "I'm not quite getting you, mister . . ." A voice that seemed to come from inside his head and chest spoke to him.

"He is Pirah, Mr. President, master of the Mystic arts, mentor to those that have ruled over five ages on the face of Earth Mother, creator of harmony between the Mystical beasts and those that would call themselves human. He has many names—the first, the keeper of balance, the destroyer of destroyers, the old one, to name a few." The president looked at the man in the chair, who had not spoken at all, then felt a presence behind him. There where once stood the fern in the large barrow sat a shaggy huge creature, legs crossed in lotus position, paws folded, with a quite human-looking face and a calm Buddha-like grin.

The president thought that the man in the chair was some incredible anomaly, but now he simply couldn't believe his eyes. He turned back to the fellow he had been talking to with a shocked look on his face and pointed at the shaggy form on the other side off the room; Pirah didn't miss a beat. "May I now introduce one of my oldest friends and allies, Mr. President? He is Lord Alitius, highest of the Terran bipeds on the North and South American continents in some cultures, a king, but he does not see himself as such. He is the steward of all things that grow, be it here or anywhere actually. Not to mention he and his enormous broods have been successful at driving this age of humans to near madness trying to find him, but you just witnessed why that is nearly impossible unless he or his fellow Sasquatch willed it." The president upended his glass, finishing his drink, and before he could set it down, it left his hand and floated over to the decanter that was hovering over the bar from which had been poured before. He stared at Alitius, trying to regain his ability to reason while his mind reeled with cognizant disbelief yet ever so realized that this was entirely real.

"Once more, Mr. President?" asked Pirah.

"Certainly," he replied without turning away from Alitius. The glass came back to him, and this time, he simply took it and brought it to his lips but then stopped and addressed both of them.

"You've really got to be shitting me. Bigfoot? I mean seriously, bigfoot? And you, are you some kind of character from a fantasy novel or something from a streaming service?"

"I told you he would say that, didn't I?" said Pirah. Alitius chuckled.

"It's a good thing I do not take into wagering on chance. However, I do believe he is catching on." The president tilted his head and made a gesture as though to say, "Well?" Pirah placed his glass on an end table that seemed to rise from the floor, and in the same moment, the president realized that the chair he was sitting in didn't come with the furniture in his office. Pirah motioned with his hand and created a picture frame that suspended itself between himself and the president. A stream of images began to appear in the frame of ancient buildings and beings, both human and otherwise, with glorious cities and amazing countryside.

"What you're seeing, Mr. President, are some images of the first four ages of humans, of which this fifth age is the only Mortal age of humans, the previous being immortal, however not invincible. These previous ages did live on this planet that is called Earth by your age. Those of us who have been with her since the times of old know her as Earth Mother, and we know her as a sentient being with the very power of creation, or if necessary, absolute destruction of life on her surface. I am her steward, and to answer your question, I am a sorcerer—Mystic, if you will—the first of all from the very beginning."

The president sipped his drink and looked once again at Alitius then back at Pirah. "What you're telling me is that beings, Giants, Dragons, Fairies, Elves, did at one time actually exist?" The president regained his power of reason, and his true ability was to accept a situation and pursue some sort of resolution.

"What I'm telling you, Mr. President, is that every tale that has been told, written, drawn, or painted was not only reality at one time on this Earth Mother but is true now—and will shortly come to this Mortal realm again. You see, Mr. President, all of those fantasy tales and bedtime stories that have been passed down through the tens of thousands of years that Mortal humans have lived in this age are, simply put, molecular memory of a time so far back in the history of this world that any evidence that could be measured by your best technology simply hasn't been discovered." The president sat thinking for a moment, first trying to push out the very first of his instincts, which was "This can't be true, but then again, how else do you explain these two, and how did they get in here? And then there are the floating glasses—and a living, breathing, thinking, speaking Sasquatch?"

"There is the unasked question, 'Why are you here?'" Pirah took his glass back and drank half of the contents. "We are here, Mr. President, to reconnoiter the great houses of humans and if they have been contacted by agents of—shall we say, others with decidedly invasive agendas for Earth Mother and Mortal kind."

"Others? What others?" the president asked.

"As there are always in life, dark and light, evil and good, so are there opposing energies in this situation, one being balance and the other being chaos," Alitius explained.

"Which are you two? If I might ask?"

"I am the keeper of balance. As was told earlier, Mr. President, the alterative entity would have been much more obvious by either seduction with promises of power and riches or overwhelming intimidation and terror," answered Pirah.

"As well as no choice in the matter of sides or no side to take in what is yet to come," Alitius added.

Baron Orbus sat looking at the wall in front of him with a look that spelled deep thought as well as calculation. He sipped at his drink once more then spoke. "Two questions, Lord Pirah and . . . Lord Alitius. What is it my nation can do in this? Also, what of the rest of the world?"

"At this very moment around the world, in every great house of men, this conversation is being held with those leaders that we have ascertained have not been corrupted by the others that seek to dominate the surface of Earth Mother. For your nation, Mr. President, I believe that you need to put your military forces on alert. I don't think you should try to explain. They simply need to be armed and ready."

"How will our weapons fare against the sort of abilities you and the others possess?" replied the president.

"Against beings of magic, they will have little or no effect. However, against the physical masses, they will have the same effect as on Mortals and the machinery you have created. Also, there may come a time when your weapons and technology may be altered and no longer function as you know it to," said Pirah.

"Can you be more precise, Lord Pirah?"

"Your gas discharge weapons will be turned to crossbows and medium and long bows as well as swords and spears. Your artillery will become trebuchet, ballista, and catapult. Your aircraft, although still operational, will not possess their weapons or the technology that operates them. Your and the other nations' militaries will have to adapt in real time, Mr. President so believe me when I say you need to be ready and choose a side. It is no jest."

The president looked thoughtful once again, putting together what was obviously true and what may not be with the question in mind. "What am I to do with this information?" The two beings in the room sat patiently waiting for his response but for only a moment longer, then the president spoke.

"Am I to be the one to share this with the rest of the world? Surely you must know that I will be labeled insane, and the houses will call to have me removed from office, and then more chaos will ensue once the vice president is sworn in from the opposing party that is overwrought with religious zealots claiming that it's 'God's vengeance on this administration,' and on and on."

Alitius looked to Pirah and tilted his head as Pirah nodded in agreement. "Mr. President, this conversation is happening at this very moment in every nation that holds power in the world of Mortals that exist on the face of Earth Mother by those that ally themselves with me and the hierarchy of the selected sovereign that is Lady Rhona of Avalon. The other leaders of the great houses of men are, at this moment, faced with the same realizations that you are having now, although I would wager that most of them aren't taking it with the same cool, thoughtful approach that you are. That all being said, Mr. President, you have much to think about, and if you feel it a good course of action, discuss it with your cabinet. Lord Alitius and I must leave you now, for the others that we spoke of have placed their masses in position and are preparing to make themselves known." Pirah stood from his chair and made a slight motion with his hand, opening then closing it to a fist. The chair and the end table next to it sank into the floor and became part of the carpet. Alitius stood up, and the president was struck at how large he actually was, standing nearly half a man taller than the president and Pirah and at least four feet wide. Alitius bowed to the president, as did Pirah. The president, having greeted royalty many times, bowed as well.

"Shall I call for an escort to show you out from one of the hidden exits?"

Pirah smiled and said, "That won't be necessary."

He then moved his right hand in an oval motion and created a ripple effect in thin air that grew to the size of Alitius's dimensions, then stopped causing an opening in what seemed like a veil that revealed some other room elsewhere. Pirah glanced at the president then motioned Alitius to walk through, then he followed. He stood watching as the portal closed, leaving no trace. The glass that Pirah drank from was back in its place, as if it had not moved at all. His drink, however, was right where he put it, and he took it and finished it in one gulp. He went to pour another when his intercom buzzed, and his private secretary came over the speaker.

"Mr. President, you are wanted in the Oval Office for a meeting with the joint chiefs and apparently NATO."

"Say that again, Gwen?" he said.

"NATO, Mr. President, and as we speak, the premier of the PRC and the president of Russia."

The president swore under his breath. "Shit."

"I think you better get a move on, sir. Now the Asia Pacific are also checking in on this meeting on video in the Oval Office."

The president acknowledged and put his coat back on. Just before leaving his office, he thought, "Everyone with a bomb or trying to get one." He then proceeded to the Oval Office, only this time, he was escorted by four Secret Service men and four Marines armed with M4 carbines. He knew what was about to happen after Pirah had told him that every "great house of man" was having the same conversation as he was with other emissaries at the same time. He came to the door of the Oval Office, where four more Marines were standing at attention as he and the rest approached. The master sergeant to the right of the president opened the door, and he entered the room to see all of the chiefs of staff as well as the attorney general, head of the FBI, and DHLS waiting anxiously. President Orbus motioned for the secretary of Defense to approach him. He leaned into him and whispered, "Put every base on the planet on full combat alert, now. I don't have time to explain, but it's about to hit the fan in a real big way."

The secretary of Defense nodded and took out his cell phone while motioning for the joint chiefs to him. A video camera was set up at the president's desk at the center of the room, while the massive screen used for conferences had been activated, and several "tiled" sections had been created with the real-time video of the president's opposite numbers across the globe looking back at him. "Mr. President, if you will?" the senior White House adviser motioned to the chair behind the desk.

"Thanks, Bill," said the President as he crossed the office and sat down.

The president looked up at the screen, and at once, the president of Russia jumped in with all the intensity of an enraged bear. *"What exactly is this?"* His question was echoed by the entire paneled screen of leaders, each with a translation being posted on their respective feeds. Systematically, each audio was muted because of the hysteria that had gripped these world leaders, and only a few were retaining their faculties and not losing their composure. One of such was the prime minister of the United Kingdom, whose demeanor seemed to never change regardless of circumstance. The others were France, Germany, Japan, New Zealand, and Australia. China, although present in the meeting, chose to go dark yet could hear and respond.

"Ladies and gentlemen, if you could please calm yourselves so there can be dialogue about this incredible, unforeseeable event that we all have just experienced," President Orbus stated. The translation bars continued to post what the leaders were saying as the president was speaking, each wanting answers immediately, if not sooner. Baron Orbus unmuted the prime minister of the UK and began to speak. "Alistair, what was your experience with this, and have you taken action yet?"

"First of all, Mr. President, we've an invested guest in this conversation, if you please." The screen split, showing an elderly woman in a different room decorated in such a way that it could only be Buckingham Palace.

"Greetings, Your Majesty, always a pleasure to see you even under the most trying of circumstances," expressed President Orbus.

"Likewise, Mr. President," replied the queen with just the hint of a smile.

Alistair Townsend, the prime minister of the United Kingdom, resumed the conversation. "In answer to your question, Baron, I was visited, as you were and all the rest, by some characters from some of the tales we were shown as children and so forth that seem to possess magical abilities and are thousands of years old and traveled from, of all places, Avalon, bloody Avalon! Excuse my language, Your Majesty." She shrugged. "One being a beautiful woman with an Arabic name of Lady Badi Ah Aziza of Avalon and somewhere called Argain, and by the way, she was nearly two meters tall, perhaps a little more, and she had the most lovely fragrance about her, and her description defies imagination. So I won't take up too much time with that, and she's accompanied by another individual, not quite so tall but a very interesting man by the name of Lord Alduriil, also of Avalon. Apparently, this fellow is a sorcerer in service of someone named Lord Pirah, the first, whoever that is, who also is in service to Avalon and the lady of the lake. Yes, that. Baron, I'm convinced that this may be true and that we may be in over our collective heads if we go at this without aligning ourselves with these people—or beings, I suppose we should refer to them as. I've informed all of our military and intelligence people to be on alert and prepare to react to especially unseemly circumstances. Not sure what else to do."

The leaders of the other nations had fallen silent during this conversation, being able to hear the exchange and each having had the same experience yet with different actions or none at all. The translation bars began to respond with a mix of statements from the other leaders, with the common thread being disbelief, that it was an elaborate hoax, and that only the first world powers could have executed such a thing while others laid the plot on the laps of the elite wealthy in an attempt to create chaos and end up with the better part of the globe dependent on privatized government. The panels began to close until only one stayed on.

"Mr. Primer? Have you anything to add?" asked President Orbus.

"We most emphatically agree with the British prime minister, President Orbus. We have had our meeting with these beings from our own lore, and we have experienced somewhat more than the rest."

The panel closed, and the screen was nearly empty except for the countries that understood the ramifications of what had occurred. President Barron Orbus sat in his chair behind the presidential desk of the Oval Office, his fingers gently touching one another in an almost reverent position. He stared at the screen and said to no one in particular, "It's about to hit the fan in a real big way."

CHAPTER 10

A Reckoning, a God Crushed, an Unholy Alliance

Her eyes were deep blue and her olive skin glistened in the midmorning sun that bathed her nudity as she lay down on the chase lounge at the balcony of the hotel room where she was staying in Volos, Greece. Calliope Andrianakis was an American-born woman from parents of Greek descent, father of Australian Greek lineage and mother born in Greece then immigrated to the US, both attending college in Orange County, California. She often dreamed of visiting the country of her family's origins and one day made that reality. She bought a ticket, took two weeks' vacation pay, and with a brand-new passport, flew off to see what this wonderful place looked like and experience what life in Greece would bestow upon her.

Her upbringing was modest but not poor as her mother and father worked hard and made sure she was well cared for and educated, including speaking fluent Greek and Latin, which came in handy in college while pursuing her degrees in world history and sociology. She lay there basking in the Aegean sun, feeling the warmth seeping into her bones and working its way to her pleasure centers, filling her head with ideas of erotic self-indulgence and causing a sly smile to appear on her sensual mouth. She raised her knees until her feet were nearly to her buttocks, then spread them apart, putting her heels together, fully exposing the area of her sex to the sun. This heightened her sexual stimulation, and she gently ran her fingers down until she felt the three-inch long and quarter-inch-wide strip of pubis that ended at the clitoral hood opening of her labia. On either side of her pubic bone were filigree tattoos augmenting her well-toned lower abdominal region. She was just about to start her fantasy foreplay when she saw a seagull floating on the wind just twenty or more feet from the rail of the balcony, staring right at her as if it knew what she was up to. She looked at the bird floating effortlessly and raised one eyebrow, then said to herself, "Never had an audience before. Enjoy." She continued with the self-play, running her fingers on either side of her sex, enjoying the slight tickling sensation.

With her eyes slowly closing, she felt the moist inner labia, rolling her hips up almost instinctively. She was just about to flirt with her clitoris when she felt a presence on the deck of the balcony with her. She opened her eyes and was immediately shocked to see a man standing there where once there was no one. She grabbed her towel on a small table next to her chaise to cover herself but found herself also mesmerized by the beautiful man who stood before her. The thought of screaming for help had somehow been wiped from her mind, and her shock did nothing to qualm her eroticized clitoris; in fact, she found herself extremely aroused and, with a certain amount of deliberation, allowed her towel to slip down and reveal her pert, glistening breasts. The man standing before her had piercing light-blue eyes, not quite as deep as hers but very compelling; his clothing was of a loose cloth, off-white, and his trousers came only to his midcalf. His shirt was fastened by small bowknots from the collar down to his waist, with just enough sheerness to the fabric that she could make out his physique and the quantity of his manhood. He had dark curly hair, much like most of the men of the region, yet he had no facial hair, which made it difficult to determine his age. "Is he twenty-seven or forty-seven?"

Those thoughts disappeared when he began to speak and stepped toward her. "Be not afraid, beautiful lady. I am here as you summoned and before you as you directed."

She looked at him and muttered, "I don't understand?"

He sat down on the chaise next to her and put his left hand at her waist and the other at the back of her head, pulling the hair clip from the bun that held the sun-kissed long brown hair that fell to her midback and over her shoulders, falling to either side of her breasts. "You will soon enough, my dear. For now let us both do as you said. Let us enjoy."

He looked into her eyes, and she couldn't control herself and pulled at the bows that held his shirt together and pulled it down, exposing a perfectly chiseled body; she inhaled his fragrance, and in her mind, she said, "Greek God if there ever was one." She took his head in her hands and pulled him to her, pressing her lips to his and shoving her tongue in his mouth. He threw back the towel, gently pushed her back on the chaise, and began to kiss her abdomen while lightly caressing her breasts, working his way down to her groomed pudenda. She let out a gasp that turned to a moan when she felt his tongue make contact with her sex. She lay back in absolute bliss, all the while thinking, "How can this be happening? It's like something out of a trash novel or a Greek fairy tale."

She reached climax after climax until she just couldn't take it anymore; she pushed him away with her heels and stood him up, pulling his trousers down and beholding his engorged penis that was truly a testament to his possible "godhood," and without a second thought, she took it with both hands and reciprocated to him the pleasure he had just bestowed upon her. In what seemed to be a never-ending cycle, he would orgasm again and again in her mouth, to the point of his seed leaking from her and running down her breasts and stomach. This time it was his turn to pull her away, and he bid her to roll over. She did without hesitation, thinking he was going to enter her in her favorite position, but the foreplay had yet to end as he treated her to his tongue once again, only it was her anus that received pleasure.

She moaned just a little louder with this as he took his time and used his forefinger with apparent skill and experience, massaging her G-spot once again, sending her into more orgasmic bliss. He paused only for her to catch her breath, and just as she did, he entered her just slowly enough for her feminine sex to adjust to his girth and length, and again the moaning became loader. They rode each other back and forth for what was indeed hours, each one climaxing over and over. He entered her anus, and she could not believe how he could bring her to climax with such intensity, and she demanded more—and more.

When they finally stopped for the evening, it was indeed the next morning, not quite before sunup. He stood in the morning quiet, his body covered with perspiration from both bodies, his erection finally settling yet still glistening from her fluids. She asked, "What do I call you? Who are you?" As the questions came out of her mouth, the seduction began to wear off, the fantasy became reality, and she became frightened.

The man looked at her, and his eyes turned to the color of lightning, and he said, "I am Zeus, God above the Gods of Olympus, and this shall be a fond memory." She was about to speak, and as she did, he leaped from the balcony, and before he dropped, he transformed into seagull and flew away. She fell back onto the chaise and fell asleep; the towel pulled itself over her to keep her warm, and the voice of Zeus spoke to her. "Sleep, my lady, and fear nothing, for you have the favor of the Gods."

Hades stood in the middle of the diocese, where the Gods of Olympus would meet encircled by the white marble chairs, each with its own cushion by their desires. Having summoned the Gods, he waited with little to no patience, expecting them to gather as they would for his brother, but lo, they did not. For more times than not, he had incurred the wrath of Zeus as well as the other high Gods of Olympus and was punished. He had been warned by Persephone, obligated wife of the lord of the Underworld, to not once again bring on the anger of his brother, or it will only turn out as before—badly for him.

The Gods began to filter in, some materializing, others actually walking in, while some flew in with their consorts in tow. Hermes took up his place next to the throne of Zeus, just behind Hera, however, who chose to stride in with her compliment of warriors, as she put it, but all knew the true nature of this male and female entourage. She walked directly past Hades and gave him a flirtatious smirk while adjusting her extremely low-positioned gown of such fabric that one could see her entire form beneath it. As Hera approached her throne next to that of the king of the Gods, all rose until she was seated. Several minutes passed as all waited for mighty Zeus to arrive, which didn't seem to bother anyone, as this was customary for their king and has been so since the dawn of the Gods. Hades looked about and came to the end of his patience.

"Hail, Gods of Olympus. I have called you here for a purpose!" The Gods stopped talking among themselves long enough to look toward Hades, then to Hera, then back to Hades, and one by one, they all began to grin and laugh as if some sort of joke had been played at his expense. Hades began to fume and transformed to a Demon with huge leather wings and a fearsome head, with menacing horns and great arms and claws of steel and a long tail that lashed about as he stood on cloven hooves and muscular legs.

He roared thunderously to a point of causing a wind form, his lungs blowing trays and foodstuffs all about the diocese. "Very well, great Hades, you have our attention. However, I need to inform you that we are here at the command of your brother and king, mighty Zeus of Olympus," said Artemis as she sorted through her quiver of arrows. Hades was about to roar once again when there was a blinding bolt of Lightning shot across the great room that held the diocese, and all stood up and bowed, for the highest of Gods on Olympus had entered, and he was indeed unhappy. He stood at the entrance of the diocese of the Gods, dressed in only a loincloth and sandals; his hair, so very thick and curly, fell below his shoulders and blended with his equally curly beard. His eyes were gray, not quite light blue, and yet had a raging fire in them; he had configured his form to be at least five times larger than the rest of the Gods in the room, putting him at the same height as his brother Hades, who had made himself ominous as to incite fear among those present, but to no avail, for they all knew that Zeus would not permit it.

Mighty Zeus strode to his brother and looked him in the eye. In his right hand he held his scepter; at the end was the symbol of his power, the lightning bolt that was the punishment to those that angered him. All the Gods stood waiting for a command from their king, but there was only silence that seemed to go on for an eternity, which, in any other circumstance, would not bother any of the Gods but what may been occurring at this very time. Hades exhaled a noxious fume from his nostrils that encircled his brother's head and covered his face; casually, Zeus simply blew the vile cloud from him and made his breath smell of flowers and honey.

"Did you not receive my message, brother?" growled Hades in his Demon form as he beat his wings and lashed his tail in a menacing display of arrogance and defiance to the diocese as well as his brother.

"I did, lord of the Underworld, and after reading it, I incinerated it, for you do not have the place in this hall of Gods to summon a gathering of such importance. Only *I* do, for I, and not *you*, am king."

Hades whipped his tail, causing a great *crack* at its end that reverberated through the hall; he then spoke. "Am I not of this diocese, brother? Do I not have my say here?"

Zeus looked at his brother evenly for what seemed an inordinate amount of time then said, "You would indeed, brother, if you would but attend from time to time. It is known that when you do make an appearance, it is but to make some sort of complaint about something or another."

Zeus continued. "You do not come to the diocese of the Gods to conduct affairs of the Underworld, as do the rest of the Gods in their own realms that they are patronized in, even though most of humankind have been intimidated into the ideology of the Nazarene and the other named prophets of that time. But if you had been paying attention, my dear brother, you would see that many have held true the Gods of Olympus as well as the Gods of other lands from the days of the first ages of humans. Do you not receive the souls that paid the ferryman to bring them to the shores of the Underworld? Does Charon not line his pockets and fill his coffers with coins proffered to him by those that have passed?" Hades glared at Zeus and shared the same menacing look to every God of the diocese of Olympus, then addressed his brother.

"Enough!" bellowed Hades, and as one, all the Gods withdrew from the semicircle, fading from view then rematerializing seated behind the throne of Zeus and Hera, on a polished stone bleacher out of harm's way. Things were about to escalate in devastating proportions.

Zeus made no threatening gesture, nor did he change his demeanor; his scepter remained lowered, and he slowly shifted his weight onto his left leg in an indifferent manner. He then addressed Hades very coolly. "Dear brother, I once again, as before, offer you this moment to join the diocese and be as the rest of the Gods with honor and reverence. Fill your seat, and be as your siblings in this very hall, joining us in what has become the change of an age."

"I did not come here to be patronized, brother, or submit to you. I came here to demand the return of the heroes of ancient Greece to the Underworld, where they became my charges, never to leave, and yet they escaped to return to the world of Mortals, taking up with others. And then there is the waif brat whom I entrusted with my guardian, Cerberus, who facilitated the escape behind my back. I want her and my pet returned with her as a captive soul, not as a servant. I want them returned *now*!" Once again, he shook the hall with his defiant roar.

"They have gone, brother, to serve those who would align themselves with the Avalon in the strife that has brought ill times to the Mystic realm, or have you been too occupied to see this in your dark kingdom?" said Poseidon from the middle tier of the bleacher. Hades could contain himself not a second more; he beat his great wings and inhaled, filled his lungs, and blew forth green flames from his stomach, spewing forth and clinging to the marble walls and pillars of the great hall within the Parthenon that housed the diocese. The Gods sat unmoving, for his powers held no sway behind the throne of Zeus and Hera. As for the queen of the Gods, she found the whole incident amusing, wondering if Hades might prevail and if she would seduce him and be the most powerful of the Gods. Zeus was somewhat difficult with this, for he had various desires that Hera simply could not keep up with.

Zeus made no effort to quench the flames and only stood for a moment, then spoke. "So be it."

Mighty Zeus created a great flash of lightning that blinded all in the room but for moment, and when they could all see again, there he stood with his magnificent armor that only the king of Olympus could create; he had no shield or sword, only his staff, which was now a bolt of lightning that defined his rightful place as the most powerful of the Gods. Hades closed his wings about him for a moment, then spread them wide in a great flurry, revealing his weapons and his signature helmet that was his power. He drew his word and bolstered his shield, his yes burning from under the nose guard of his helmet. Zeus himself had also taken a guarded stance, his eyes turning to bright blue-gray orbs as the two began their single combat dance, one taking a step as the other did the same. Hades advanced with a powerful downward slash to head of Zeus, only to be parried by his staff. Then he made another attempt at his shoulder, and once again, to no avail, Zeus sidestepped, then whirled out of reach, only to bring down his lightning bolt to the shield now covering the upper body of Hades, smashing his brother to the floor.

Hades pushed himself to his feet with his wings then beat them, lifting him out of reach of the next strike brought on by his brother—but only for a second as mighty Zeus leaped forward and brought a crushing blow to the head of Hades and shattered his prized helmet, the signet of his realm. The king of the Underworld reeled back in half consciousness as the blow had struck home and rendered him senseless. Once again he hit the floor, only this time with greater force than before, leaving him motionless for a moment as Zeus approached him and stood over his dazed brother. "Again, you lose your temper in this hall, and again you are dashed to floor as if you could not foresee this outcome, just as it has occurred time and time again throughout the ages of the Gods."

Hades began to stir, and his terrifying form simultaneously transformed back to the human appearance before his tantrum began. He stood trying to assume some sort of dignity, but Zeus was not finished; his armor vanished, leaving him once again with only his loincloth and sandals, and his scepter had changed back to a staff. Yet he remained gigantic in the center of the hall. His eyes still glowed as his temper had not subsided, and his mind had been made up to cease this once and for all. "You, Hades, God of the Underworld, are as of this moment banished from Olympus for eternity and shall never, as long as the greater powers look upon us, seat at the diocese of the Gods." With that Zeus walked over to the marble chair that was the place kept for his brother and, with one blow of his great fist, crushed the chair into rubble.

He then looked to Hades and, with a look of complete indifference, said, "Be gone." At that moment, Aeolus stood from his place at the bleacher and thrust forth his right hand, causing a whirlwind to appear around Hades and engulf him, taking him from the hall and back from whence he came.

"So now we are set to this thing," said Poseidon.

Zeus, without looking toward his sibling, simply nodded and said, "Yes."

The great doors of the entrance to the throne room of the Underworld burst open as Hades stormed in, having been deposited at the gates to his realm, where there was no three-headed guardian to greet him. He motioned to one of the servants, whose eyes had been closed and sealed, to bring him some wine. The servant felt her way to a table and to a decanter and chalice, then poured her master his drink. She then carried it to him, feeling her way to where he stood. Hades felt in control in his realm and languished at the fear he created with the servants of his keep. The girl stood before him with the chalice, waiting for him to take it. As he took it, the girl breathed a quiet sigh, as did the others in the room. The mere fact that he took the chalice and didn't torment the girl was a sign that they may not be the "release" of his wrath as in times before. He looked around and did not see anyone but servants standing along the walls; he took a long draft of his wine and spoke with a harsh tone. "Where is she?"

The girl who brought his wine had not returned to her place along the wall, and she spoke in ancient Greek, "Her Majesty takes rest out on the escarpments to the north of the keep, Your Grace."

Hades looked her up and down, noticing her ample breasts, tiny waist, and taut buttocks. He created a slight breeze that pushed her dark but very sheer gown to her body, giving him a better view of her beauty. He thought, "Perhaps after my wife has retired." Then he motioned for her to refill his chalice; he looked about the room and noticed that there were no guards or courtiers that would fawn about him, and other than the blind servants, he was alone.

She brought him his wine, and just as he was about to take it, she reacted to something unseen yet felt, as did the other servants. The chalice shook in her hand, and he snatched from her. He was about to slap her to the floor for almost spilling his beverage when a voice spoke to him from behind. "Good morrow, ruler of the Underworld and newly exiled God of Olympus," came the words from an unexpected source, yet the voice was unmistakable. Hades turned to see what might be considered his opposite number in the grand scheme of things in the Mystic world—or in this case, the realm of Gods. He looked at the man and his companions that stood in the doorway of his throne room; all were interestingly beautiful, including the one who spoke to him, whom already knew, having witnessed the last five ages of life on Earth Mother himself. He also knew that it was the diocese of the Gods of Olympus that named him other than corruptor, defiler, accursed, deceiver, and many others, but the most common name he had come to be known as was Favlos, ruler of Corsolvess and self-anointed God king of such. Hades would have engaged this one for simply barging into his realm without herald or permission and might have won the battle, this being where his power was greatest, but he found himself intrigued by this unexpected visit. Favlos stood with his tiny consort and four others of similar dimensions all just behind him, as well as some other interesting beings of omnisexual disposition, and not one was armed or looked ominous in the least.

"How did you get in here, and furthermore, why did you come, Lord Favlos?"

Favlos made a gesture to ask for some wine, and Hades motioned to the same servant, who then poured and brought the chalice to the accursed, who also looked the girl up and down, then said, "Blinding them? I never thought of that. How defiantly delicious. I must give one a go sometime."

"Perhaps later. Now will you answer me why you have come, and there is the question of your entrance," stated the Underworld king.

Favlos took a small, almost dainty sip of his wine, then said to his host, "As I stated before, newly exiled God of Olympus, I believe you and I and some other deities of old have a common situation, that if we were to combine our great resources, we could find ourselves in a much more . . . commanding situation?" Hades grinned and chuckled, with no evidence of thinking in the same resonance of this Mystic of a far-off realm. "I am not unaware of your history, Lord Favlos. Your list of attempts do not show any victories, save for preserving Corsolvess from complete destruction."

"If you don't mind, Your Grace, I am addressed as Holiness, as I have been made a God in my own right." Hades looked at the Mystic again, only this time, the curiosity was nowhere to be found. His eye once again began to glow, and all his servants cowered to the walls, expecting terrible feats of godly power to be unleashed in the room. Yet Hades restrained himself then spoke. "Since I am the only deity within these walls save my wife and my children, I believe I will decide what to call you."

Favlos knew he had to be diplomatic, for indeed, within this realm, Hades's power was supreme. Even Mighty Zeus would not have engaged him or other Gods in their own realm, much less their own keep. "Yes, well, allow me to regale you with the current situation, Your Grace. You see, I've launched a rather intricate campaign in the realm of Mystics as well as on the face of Earth Mother, a campaign that may interest you as the outcome does not exist, only the continued chaos that Dark Lords like yourself and someone else you might want to meet find ever so beautiful and destructive with no end, ever as there is no final battle, only skirmishes and plunder and mayhem—beautiful, massive-scale mayhem."

"Who is this that I would like to meet exactly?"

Another voice from the other side of the great doors spoke as the other stepped from just to one side of the entrance. "Someone who has been compared to you as you have been compared to me for as long as Gods have been Gods," said the man dressed in Nordic chain mail and sporting a cape of black and green fur and fabric, with black leather trousers and a great master belt that sported two long daggers with Nordic carvings on the pommels. His hair was long and black and fell to his midback and chest, with braids and ornaments weaved into them. He wore finely crafted boots that laced up just before his knees. His vanity and his swagger complimented his surroundings, and Hades knew who he was at the sight of him.

"Welcome to the Underworld, Loki, the trickster."

CHAPTER 11

Student, Disciple, Lord

San Diego, a city that lay at the very southwest corner of the US and resting on the coast of the Pacific Ocean, giving the mystic a wonderful place to go and have wonderful time, and to an extent, this was true. But for others of this time, it was not to be wonderful, for the world of Mortals was about to explode and be driven back into an age so long forgotten that the stories of those times had become fantasy and lore—or even fairy tales.

In a loft apartment situated in the Gaslamp district of this city, there lived a man whose story went with every fantasy and story told to children at bedtime for two ages of life on the face of Earth Mother. Though you will not see his name in any book, you wouldn't hear it said in any story spoken of but perhaps in mention only.

He went by Tarot, a psychic greater than most and unknown to the greater masses yet sought out by the powerful and discreet. He stood at his window, looking out at the people who passed, yet did not notice them, for he already knew about the visitor that would be coming to him, and it involved the enormous changes that were about to overtake every last soul that walked below—as well as all who lived on the face of Earth Mother. He waited patiently, as he had done for many lifetimes of humans and others who would seek his abilities. He turned and walked to his high-backed leather chair in the center of his expansive loft that served as his sanctum and the core of his powers. He looked at his watch and said, "Good evening, my lord Pirah. Please come in."

Tarot motioned with his right forefinger, and the door latch rotated to the unlock position, and the door swung open. From outside the door, Pirah strode in and looked about the walls and the flooring as well as the bed and living area, all reminding him of the third and fourth ages of human life on Earth Mother. "I love your décor, Tarot. It reminds me of great and wondrous times."

Tarot stood and greeted Pirah in the ancient fashion of clasping arms, and they stood looking at each other, for indeed it had been quite long since they had seen each other. "They are still great and wondrous times, my lord. They are simply not *these* times. More's the pity," replied Tarot. He motioned for Pirah to be seated in an identical chair just across him, with a table between them that had been set with a cocktail service, two glasses, and a bottle of expensive vodka.

Tarot took the bottle and poured both of them a drink, and they touched glasses before taking a sip. "I'm sure you knew I was coming tonight, but I don't think you know exactly what for, my friend."

Tarot tilted his head with a questioning look on his face. "Do you not come for my allegiance in the coming chaos? The accursed launches an after attack. I think I could be helpful in this."

Pirah interjected. "Indeed helpful, and your allegiance was never questioned in my heart. I have simply come to tell you that your time as disciple has ended. I have come to bring forth that which has been earned over two ages of humans and thousands of years of study and practice. I have come to tell you, Tarot, that you are to be fully anointed as a Mystic and master of your craft." Pirah stuck out his palm, and a wonder tendril emerged and made its way to Tarot's forehead. He felt the energy coming from Pirah, his teacher, his master, the one who took him in as a mortal, showed him the ways, and discovered his intuitive abilities that were far and above many that called themselves psychic.

As this conjuring went on, Tarot beheld his life as it was in the beginning and how it manifested today. He could see the failures that were actual blessings, that he could change his thinking and his direction, and how he bestowed this upon those that sought him out for council. He recalled the many times he had fallen in love with Mortal women after he himself had become immortal and how he suffered when they finally transitioned to the next life. He could see those that he had mentored and brought into their ability; some went on to do well, others became self-seeking and untruthful. These he was obligated to remove from the populace by redirection or sometimes single combat, never to be heard from again. All these experiences brought him to this moment.

Pirah pulled back the tendril and took a deep breath while Tarot sat with his eyes closed, still entranced by the experience that just transpired. He then opened his eyes, and the slightest of grins appeared in a very crooked lower corner of his mouth, and he said, "I had no idea this was happening tonight, my lord Pirah. I am stunned and without words."

Pirah stood, and with his drink in his hand, he said, "Rise, Lord Tarot, Mystic of the realm, and lord of Avalon." Tarot rose to his feet with his drink in hand, and they touched glasses once more and downed their drinks. "Congratulations, my lord, you have earned this many times over, and you should be just a touch prideful—though that has never been the case for you."

"I am honored, my lord, truly," Tarot replied with a slight bow of his head as Pirah placed his glass on the table and added, "As you may have felt, your powers have become greater than before. However, you still only have limited abilities outside of your keep, as you have been since you were a disciple."

"Understood, my lord," acknowledged Tarot.

"You will have your full intuitive ability, which is still quite formidable, but still, to defend yourself, you must remain ready with conventional Mortal means that you have been using to this very day. Know this, my lord. As time passes, that limitation will diminish, and you will be able to wield the full capacity of your power anywhere on the face of Earth Mother or the Mystic realm, but you must be patient."

"Of course, my lord, I understand fully. And waiting for a moment is something you have taught me well and has come in quite beneficial over the centuries, is it not?"

Pirah looked in his eyes and spoke, "Nevermore do we need insight than the days ahead, my lord, and so I must be off, for there are more visits to old friends and students, and there is simply no time. When you are called, I have but one request."

"What would that be, beloved Pirah?"

"Be ready."

Lo, good reader, the journey continues as the two realms of Mortal and Mystic intertwine in the next installation The Chronicles of Pirah: *The Change of an Age and the Rise of the Seer.*

www.ingramcontent.com/pod-product-compliance
Lightning Source LLC
LaVergne TN
LVHW091557060526
838200LV00036B/887